RHP

TELL IT NOT

SEVENTEEN STORIES

by

Deborah Freeman

TELL IT NOT: Seventeen Stories by Deborah Freeman
ISBN 978-0-9855199-6-4
First edition. Copyright © 2022 by Deborah Freeman

Published in the United States of America by
Red Heifer Press
410 Oakwood Court
Tehachapi, California 93561-1943

Cover art: "Self-Portrait with Brush and Palette" (detail)
by Artemisia Gentileschi (1593-1653)
Cover and Book Design by Red Heifer Press.
Graphic artwork by Charles Vaught.
Printed in the United States of America.

The paper used in this publication meets the minimum requirements of American National Standard of InformationSciences—Permanence of Paper for Printed Library Materials. ANSI/NISO Z39.48-1992.

To my husband, my sons,
my daughters in law, and
all our grandchildren.

Contents

Apron

The stories in this collection cover 43 years. "The Lizard" was first sketched in 1978, "Verity Thomas" was written in 2021. Some of the stories are linked by recurring themes, which reflect some of the recurring themes of my life.

D.F.

The Lizard

It is August 1974. We have moved from our three-roomed third-storey immigrant flat to this dilapidated villa, one of the original Ashkelon cottages of twenty years ago, when the State of Israel could hardly afford bricks, let alone mortar. Four tiny rooms, a kitchen with standing room only, every doorpost or window ledge rotted by woodworm. (It takes us a while to recognize that fuzzy brown lines snaking up walls are woodworm colonies.) In our tiny garden a streetlight grows up through the branches of a tree, encircled by frantic bats. There is the sweet suffocating odour of guavas, which will rot on the sandy ground until the school-children start to come, collecting them for the soldiers, somewhere in the desert.

Two small children, a third on the way. The lavatory – a necessary appendage at any time, but with small babies more valuable than twenty trips to a zoo – blocked. Our landlord assures us the black stuff in the bottom of the lavatory will come off with bleach, and suggests we probably use it too much.

We sit in the garden on the cracked wall, suck at sweet peaches, and watch a giant cockroach perched near us, its antennae waving. The cockroach family has been around three hundred and fifty million years longer than the family of man. I guess they are at a high level of awareness.

It is from within this morose scene that we first set eyes on Margaret and Simon, our neighbours. The cottages adjoin, the lawn (ours overgrown and yellow, summer scrub, theirs clipped short and sprayed green,) in common, and the roofs made of the same grey tiles. Under one of those tiles, a pigeon will get trapped one day. Their children, watched by ours, will scramble up onto the roof, remove the tile and set it free; but that comes later in the story. Later, after Margaret has dreamed that a mystical Rabbi arrives, and stands astride our two rooftops, trying to say something. Later, after a winter where rain drips over the leaves in our gardens, and makes the coarse grass green again.

They stand on their veranda, he in white shorts and shirt, she with a yellow "alice band" across her hair. They're here to breathe the night air, not to inspect us. But seeing us, they're welcoming enough. His voice is a cello, hers a viola.

And my growing writing habit! Our very first night, I take out a notebook, and write.

> Our neighbours are psychologists. They are new to Israel as we are, trying to come to terms with whatever Israel is to the English-speaking Jew. I dictate to myself a writers exercise. I shall put them down on paper. I shall ignore

cockroaches and dirt. I love my babies for having brought me to this house – car-free paths for them to walk and play on, lined with sycamore trees and bushes - and I shall write day after day.

Except of course, it isn't going to happen. The writing exercise, or whatever I mean by it. Life is too busy.

How weird were our first few nights. We spent them trying to get used to the feeling of open skies outside the front door, instead of a stone landing opposite a neighbour's metallic front door. We had one more room than we'd had in our cramped flat, but all the rooms were smaller. We moved on the night of a full moon. The August wind blew hotly across it, stifling, yet boding the arrival of the first damp moments of blessed autumn.

After those first nights, the tensions under which we had been living, moving countries, having babies, a cramped flat, began to dissolve themselves, as the freedoms of grass and trees, not to mention the smell of the sea made themselves felt. We turned into each other's arms, and made love in a way we hadn't for weeks before. Next morning we helped our children out of their cots and let them roam free, in the garden. In no time they were hunting beetles, tasting leaves, while the little one, not yet standing attempted to pull himself up by means of the crumbling wall.

In September came Rosh Hashanah, Jewish New Year. The season of forgiveness, and reckonings. Our Hebrew was good enough to follow radio phone ins on the topics, and these reminded me of a mix of Christmas and Easter back in England.

My desire to get to know our neighbors grew. Brief exchanges didn't satisfy me. On the night of Rosh Hashanah itself, curiosity defeated me. Nine in the evening, I crept outside in my nightie, to peep through their shutters. It was windy, and the nightie flapped in the breeze. They were sitting round their table, with its white table-cloth and candlesticks. Margaret was freshly showered and glowing, Simon's hair was brushed back, which made him look older. His feet were bare under the table. The children, a son and a daughter, talked animatedly.

"I heard something," the little boy insisted, his sunburnt face turning from one to the other. "Why do you say I didn't hear anything? Through my wall."

"What exactly did you hear?" asked Simon.

"Someone talking, then crying. Then praying to God."

I smiled in the warm night, and felt embarrassed. At the same time grinning in the dark. I crept through our garden, back to home base.

§

From the start Simon spoke more with Adam than with me. He commuted to Jerusalem three days a week, complaining that the climb through the Jerusalem hills gave him earache. The change in air pressure . . .

What was it I wanted from him and from Margaret, who would come to sit on our cracked wall carrying her coffee mug, gravely relaxed after her day's work in a local school? She enjoyed helping children with handicraft and painting.

"There is something about Margaret, about both of them, that's hard to put into words," I found myself observing to Adam.

"Normal people," he commented, "don't worry about how to put everything into words."

"I think . . ." I tried to find a shape for my feelings, ". . . if I could see where they have come from and where they are going, I would understand my own journey better. Our journey. Perhaps, through them I am seeking a deeper understanding of Israel, of our having come here."

"When you go shopping," was his response, "get some more olives."

§

Margaret returns one hot afternoon from Migdal, previously the Arab village of Majdal. The downtown of Ashkelon, crowded home to Jewish immigrants from Morocco and Algeria. Her arms are loaded with fruits and vegetables. Behind her a trail of flowers and brightly coloured plastic sheeting for a new shower curtain. She observes sadly, "Those poor men, all with wooden legs or crutches, squatting on every sidewalk and selling cheap plastic."

Walking through Migdal is an experience that leaves anyone exhausted. Through the main street, old new and even older blend with Middle Eastern flavourings. A stainless-steel counter with a modern refrigerator and a huge printed notice. G'lida (ice-cream) is the frontage of one shop, whose old and wrinkled shopkeeper pats g'lida into cornets with his fingers, then wipes his hands on his filthy overall or licks them with a youthful tongue. The walls of his shop are painted pale blue to ward off the evil eye. The streamlined look of the shop contrasts with its shriveled occupant. The pervading smell is of sweat and of the olives that he keeps in a cracked saucer next to the cash-register and chews from time to time with chunks of pitta bread.

To one side of the shopping area there are chicken and turkey shops. A turkey glares at Margaret through a smudged window.

On Thursdays the people from the agricultural settlements around Ashkelon drive donkey carts into town to sell watermelons, peaches, purple eggplants shimmering in the sun, rancid pears softened by the harsh heat, lettuces flung into green mountains, then falling, trodden underfoot, dark green parsley crushed between the boxes, everything trampled by the rush of women waving green and yellow plastic shopping bags, shrieking at the vendors in con-demnation of the quality of what they are about to buy.

"Mah?" meaning "What?" they cry, meaning how much can you possibly want for this? They press the fruit, soften it, leave it one stage further decayed for the next buyer.

Margaret walks through the market with her nose held high. She enjoys the fights that spring up, then die away: fist-fights, curses, punches, incantations.

Then, through the tides of food and people, she spies several ranges of enormous marrows, split into quarters, as if at sea, or about to set sail. A fleet of orange boats. She feels elevated, and knows she is on a journey. Sailing.

§

One afternoon, while unloading the shopping in her porch, Margaret turned to me and said, "Come with me to the park?" As if we were real friends. I said yes, of course. Adam was at home with the children.

She drove us along the coastal road that led to the park. The green, the sea, the birds, in minutes we felt refreshed. She pulled up to park beside the wooden hut of Ashkelon park's chief warden.

I had spoken with him before, but not in the way Margaret now did. She hugged him, "Hi Yossi!" I was immediately jealous. Yossi, a heavy, moustached man in his early sixties, sat in his small hut, on an uncomfortable chair covered with brown blankets. A dust-covered radio looked as if it had been left behind by the departing British army in 1948.

"Let me introduce you," Margaret said to me. I had left my bag on the back seat, and as she closed and locked the door I thought perhaps I should hide it. But I was distracted. Yossi showed Margaret his gun. She smiled benignly upon it.

"Dangerous times," she said sweetly to me. Then (how I wanted to hear from her, and how I listened!) she embarked on an account of how she and Simon had taken up arms against the shallow materialism of the New York Jewish community in which they lived, and moved to Israel. Though here, now they were finally here, it seemed different.

"The leap of faith that I had made turned out to be more than moving from one religion to another," she explained. "It meant moving countries."

§

"Who is your friend? Yossi asked her. "A tourist?" We peered inside his little hut, to watch him brewing mint tea. Three teaspoons of sugar piled into each tiny gold-rimmed glass. The walls of his sanctum were lined with pictures of half-naked women, several of these embraced by a man who looked like a younger version of himself.

"We are not tourists, Yossi. She's my neighbour!" He winked at her. He had pitted skin, and his brown eyes grazed over the two of us, but more over her than me. The car was yards away but we were leaning forward, our backs to it.

There was a smash of glass. We turned round, both of us, to see a youth scamper away from Margaret's car, glass on the ground beside it, carrying my bag.

"Hey!" Yossi shouted after the youth, who ran off up a slight slope, then away between eucalyptus trees.

"My bag!" I cried.

"My car!" Margaret added. We were shocked, both of us, it happened so quickly. And even more quickly Yossi was on the case.

"Now you must to not worry," he said calmly, speaking in English, then reverting to Hebrew, to inform me I would get my bag back, and insurance would cover the repair of Margaret's car. Gangs, he said, calmly, all over the park. He added accusingly that I shouldn't have left my bag exposed like that... "Go for walking," he said, "and when you get back, the bag will be here. If not today – tomorrow."

"Come," said Margaret authoritatively, leading me away, and we set off, as if this was a perfectly normal occurrence, into the park. We passed by palm trees, then stopped beside a deep well, which had once held water for the ancients who peopled the streets of Ashkelon. It was covered with a twentieth century iron grid, for safety.

"Margaret," I said, "We need to call the police." Then she explained how well she knew Yossi. He had come here from Turkey or from Lebanon with no wife and five delinquent sons, one of whom now ran protection rackets across Ashkelon from the shuk to the park and back again. If he said he would get my bag back then he meant it and we should trust him.

"Your car has been vandalised," I repeated stubbornly.

"Esther," said Margaret in a tone that I recognized as patronizing, "trust me."

"I trust you." (Not true at this moment.) "I don't trust him."

"We are in two different places!"

Was she trying to teach me cultural relativism?

"This guy – I know him. Simon knows him too. His stories are not like our stories. If he says he'll get your bag back, then he will."

On the rough grass four ravens strutted ceremoniously, peering imperiously out toward the sea. We were near the remains of Ashkelon's crusader fort. I imagined crusaders on horseback thundering by.

"Was there much of value in it?"

"A small amount of cash, and two spare momos."

"What are mow-mows?"

She looked quizzical, and I sensed more disconnection. Too many words that needed explanation, and here I was wanting to learn to write in the English of my childhood.

"Momo was our family name for the Hebrew word motzetz. A dummy."

"Oh! You mean a pacifier!" We finally understood each other, Margaret and I, but to no avail.

"Dummies, as you call them, do real harm to children. I can't believe you give them to your babies!"

"Only when they're going to sleep," I lied.

We left the park, having agreed with Yossi to come back at eight in the morning. Over the jagged silhouette of broken glass I watched gambolling rabbits, and caught sight of a snake speeding through grass.

"Are there dangerous snakes here, do you think?" I wanted so much to make conversation with Margaret. How she embraced this place. She began to hum "She'll be coming down the mountain when she comes..." then paused, and said, "No idea, Esther. We'll come back in the morning, eh?"

§

Next morning Adam was home to watch our babes, feasting on stoned olives and gulping their little bottles of warmed milk. The warm air blew through the broken window of Margaret's car. Ashkelon wind always smelt of the Mediterranean.

Margaret mused as we went, "I hope he turns out to be right. Do you think we should believe him? Honestly, Esther, it's that leap of faith, for me, over and over again, living here."

Normally her childhood was left out of our conversations, but not this morning.

"I was lucky. Our family priest was just like Yossi. Full of bonhomie, I mean. Flirtatious, touchy feely. But so wise! The day I told him I had lost my faith, he put a hand on my arm, looked into my eyes, and said, 'Go in peace, dear Maggie. You will find God again when the time is right.'"

Then as we got out of the car, by Yossi's hut she said, "Your Adam would have made a good Catholic. He's whimsical, ephemeral, at times - hard to grasp, know what I mean? But he's so good. Did you know that too?"

§

We came to the hut, and Yossi wasn't there. Someone else was. A taller younger man, with Yossi's grin and dark eyebrows. He spoke to us in good Hebrew, and said my bag had been located by his father, and here it was. He reached to pull it out of a drawer.

"What about what was in it?" I asked him. He shrugged, as if wasting words to answer that question was too much of an effort.

We had a beautiful walk in the park that day but I was frustrated at every turn because I wanted to gain some understanding of Margaret, but failed to do so. And that was how it went. She shared so little with me, yet continued to drop in casually, un-announced.

She knocked on the door on the evening, weeks later when Adam came home with the news that he had decided to join the army. Later still she and Simon came over together to observe as Adam emptied the contents of the large brown kitbag he had been issued with.

We sat round as a pile accumulated on the floor. Trousers which Adam found to be small, boots a bit big, white vests, and other adornments issued by the army to new arrivals. I sat with tears in my eyes envisaging him being blown up or maimed for life somewhere in the Sinai desert. I was angry because this was what he had chosen, although actually, Israel being Israel he had little choice at this time.

"Soon you can write your first really Israeli story," said Simon, himself the first of several people who would in due course tell me what I ought to write about.

"Adam in the army."

"I couldn't do that." I said to him. "That would have to be in Hebrew." I was thinking – it will be better, then if Adam gets killed while we are both still young. Then at least the children and I will have a chance to build another life. I hoped they had no idea what was in my mind. Margaret breathed in, then out, deeply.

"I just love beginnings! Esther, don't you love them too?"

And then there was the time Adam was merrily showering himself, and singing Adeste Fidelis at the top of his voice, which was melodious and deep when he was happy, wavering and tuneless when he was miserable. As he walked out of the shower, his tall brown body dripping water which flowed down onto our shabby tiles in streams as if from taps, he, blinking, making for the bedroom to get a towel, he found himself face to face with an amazed Margaret who had run in without knocking to shout:

"You sing beautifully! Lock your door when you have a shower!" and fled laughing away, while he padded across the tiles leaving footprints which soon dried in the summer air.

§

This country is an empty shell without its history. If not the history, then what are we doing, planting ourselves on these shores? Margaret loves to visit the antiquities in Ashkelon's National Park. Here old gods keep watch in stone clusters, or hide in grassy dips. Most have names I do not know. She is in love with the land. The soil, plants, animals, the climate, she studies everything with tenderness.

One afternoon she runs over to where I am sitting. "Someone I want you to meet, Esther!" I follow her back to her neat lawn, where I see a blond figure bending over Gally, their white dog, trying to take a thorn out of her paw.

"Esther, Ilana! Ilana, Esther!" she introduces us. "This amazing woman," she says, "runs hikes to exotic places, she's going to set up a natural history museum right here in Ashkelon, and she knows the names of all the wild grasses in the world!" She picks up a spray of something purple, trailing it delicately. "Not to mention birds, flowers, thistles. Yes, even thistles!"

We see a great deal of Ilana in the weeks that follow. She is a blond Israeli, with eyes which though blue have learned to withstand the harsh sunlight – I have no idea how.

A few days later, Margaret is in her garden, feet bare, regaling us with another hike she has been on with Ilana and her group. This march was across the rocky Judean desert, through dried wells, along winding side-paths, over fields of winter flowers; through the yellow abundance of mimosa trees, to the sand caves of Beit Gubrin near Ashkelon, where swarms of black ladybirds swirled, little clouds of nature, making patterns in the air before her eyes.

§

I imagined myself drawn to Margaret because of how effortlessly she seemed to have acclimatised to our new country. Myself - I didn't yet belong. Some mornings I woke to find the chirping of birds in the air sounded strange. Clouds swept over the sea in constellations I could not fathom. Children ran past our cottage on their way to school, and they looked like little ghosts from the future – unreal, and I had no idea why.

I resented her a little too, for not minding her own imperfect Hebrew, while my successful mastery of the language did the opposite of what it was supposed to do. It locked me out instead of letting me in. The more Hebrew I spoke the more I felt imperfectly connected.

Margaret did not like my reflective moods any more than Adam did, and gradually she turned for better company to our neighbours opposite. Freddy Rosenthal, and his wife Anna. Older than us, middle-European. Freddy strolled past our gardens most afternoons at five o'clock. His sunburnt face, small bald head, wrinkled shirts led me at first to take him for a gardener.

"Listening to Freddy," Margaret enthused, "is like listening to a potted history of the Jews of the twentieth century!" They had been in Germany, in concentration camps, settled in a kibbutz in the north, then broken away and come to the peace of Ashkelon where they tended their garden. Freddy played their baby grand, which took up half of their living room, Anna read books in German, English and Hebrew, and occupied herself with the underprivileged of Ashkelon, immigrants who had come from North Africa, as opposed to immigrants like herself, who had lost everything under Hitler. Freddy gave piano lessons, smoked pipes, put manure on his roses in the right season, and pruned them when necessary. Freddy and Anna's families had long complex stories of conversions, which I relished.

"The one about your cousin who became a Christian and emigrated to Turkey where he married a Muslim," I requested.

"My cousin Arik? Ah, now he's just arrived here in Israel, with his wife and children. They are in Zichron Yaakov, in the north."

"Are they becoming Jewish, then?"

"No. He has a dream to be a good German Christian here in Israel. We must allow him to try."

One day he stopped beside our wall, not Margaret's, his head tilted to one side, reminding me of the large lizard that lived close by. At the very same moment, the lizard appeared. The D.H. Laurence poem came back to me. I remembered reading it as a student, in the depths of an English university library. Back there the poem spoke to me.

"If men were as much men
As lizards are lizards,
Then they'd be worth looking at."

Under the gaze of this intellectual neighbour who knew Goethe, Schiller, every other German Romantic poet, my little quote shrivelled to insignificance. With a toss of its tail the lizard went speedily on its way, into the shade of desiccated leaves on the wall.

"Your children," Freddy observed in his German accent, "are industrious. Keeping busy is good." From then on, his air of authority led my little ones to look serious as soon as he popped his head over the wall. Bundles of stones, clusters of dead beetles, houses of sticks, whatever they were playing with would be laid out for Freddy's approval. While he surveyed their world his wife would chat with Margaret, their two curly heads, one grey one dark nodding in convivial agreement. I understood then that these two women were fast becoming friends for life, and would in due course tell each other everything.

Tell it Not

Tell it not in Gath, publish it not in the streets of Ashkelon; lest the daughters of the Philistines rejoice, lest the daughters of the uncircumcised triumph.

Book of Samuel.

I brought my wife and children here because I need a homeland a shelter an identity and them. The new flavours of a new existence. We are in Ashkelon, a small seaside town, blown by Mediterranean winds, small cottages built and built onto, stuccoed and shuttered; narrow streets lined with sycamore and eucalyptus trees, almond blossom and bougain-villea, lizards on walls prowling their territories, bats in the air on winter nights. Guava in gardens in autumn, their scent lying heavily over the neigh-bourhood, the way clouds lay over the city in England. Crickets tsip-tsipping in the sun. The whirr of low-flying dragon-flies, wings catching colour from everywhere. And the roar of low flying aircraft, silver and thunder matched together in a deadly com-bination across the sky.

We sweat here for months of the year. August we fall asleep exhausted from the heat. Where my wife's head rests on my shoulder a wet patch emerges on which she slides, until she slithers off and back onto her own pillow.

In the morning our son who is three has to go to gan. He eats a biblical breakfast - bread, milk and olives. Then I take his hand and walk him to his kindergarten, which is on the other side of the empty square in front of our house. The square had grass on it when we first came here, but it died. The place has been loaded with piles of iron rods and little hills of fresh sand and pebbles. They'll be building something here soon.

He carries a rucksack of provisions, an apple and a peanut butter sandwich, which jogs on his back. He is brave but uncertain. To him the few yards from our home to his gan seem like the world.

Now we are at the gan gate. The garden has a rusty slide, wooden swings, two sand pits, a row of tires stuck in the sand, painted yellow blue red and green. Living so near we are often early. My son greets the gannenet. Large, dark, sallow, warm, irritable. Tough. The first month I took Danny to her calmly, untroubled. We were building ourselves a new life. The heat, the pressure, the inflation, the expense of furnishing our new home. I was forgetting I was a Jew. (Wasn't that the reason we came here? So our Jewishness might blend, as opposed to stand out?) But on one day of great heat the gannenet came to greet us in the garden wearing a short-sleeved dress. As she held out her thick arms to greet my son, I saw first of all the black hairs, the rounded knuckles of her hands - then the row of numbers printed on her arm. History hit me as the gate squeaked.

In England I cultivated a kind of easy-going confusion as to what I felt – about most things. The Jewish thing for example. I quite liked to feel confused about that. So did my wife. Odd things that were supposedly to do with Jewish identity sometimes annoyed me. The fact that my parents took for granted from the day I was born that I would grow up to be a doctor. Which I did. But how I wish someone had once said, Ah, a musician, he'll be a musician. By the time I was a student, I was connecting the two things. My identity as a Jew – whatever that was - and the freedom to play my saxophone. Between those two freedoms I knew there was a deep inner sense of my own, personal freedom.

And I never dreamed that the neighbours here would be just as unreasonable as my neighbours in London. This week alone, the Yemenite policeman down the road, the librarian from Austria, the American psychologist, the sabra teacher opposite – they have taken it in turns to knock on our door to complain that my saxophone disturbs them. Personal freedom my foot.

We left London as a tide was turning. The Middle East was changing. When I was a child, my parents' conversations were about how exciting it was that Mr Brown the newsagent thought it was right for Jews to have their own country, and he wasn't even Jewish. But as I grew up I began to notice things changed. The Palestinians arrived. Of course they had always been there, one way or another. But not morally significant. For years the Arab countries were moral criminals because an infinitesimally small percentage of their incomes could have settled every Palestinian refugee in comfort forever. But now things were different. By the time I left London our friends, Jewish ones included, said the moral right of the Palestinians was as great as that of the Jews. And the Arabs were lucky to have oil as a weapon because a wrong had been done. Auschwitz or no Auschwitz right was right, wrong was wrong. Our friends gave us a great send-off, all of them, but only three of them mentioned coming to visit us. I knew that if we'd been going to a commune in California, a secluded bay in southern Cornwall, a small flat in Yugoslavia, their desire to come and experience our new life-style would have been greater.

My son's gannenet Marta seems unaware of the changes taking place in the western world. So do the dozen or so Israeli mothers who bring their children to the gan, and collect them, hearts full of love, stomachs loose in summer dresses, perspiration under their arms. They chat with each other about children, their other children, nephews, brothers, husbands away in the army. Only rarely do they discuss politics. Will there be a real peace with Egypt? Might the world come to an end? Did the children have head lice last year or was it the year before?

Recently Marta caught cystitis. She was pale under her sallow skin, and kept the gan open out of pure heroism. She sipped water regularly and grimaced between sentences. She told me that she caught cystitis the day she arrived in Israel – then Palestine.

"You won't believe it, she said proudly. "A year and a half in Auschwitz - I was healthy as a cow. When I took off what clothes I had they crawled away from me, so lice-ridden was I. And when we washed in the winter water froze on my back and made me a jacket of ice to wear. But (staring at me and I couldn't look away) the day I got here I got cystitis. I have it twice a year now, it fits into my yearly routine." She burst out laughing, along with a grimace.

The American psychologist says I should go to the municipality and ask if there are music rooms in a local school where I can practise my saxophone. He used to enjoy jazz, in Baltimore. His wife makes batiks in their garden, and stirs cauldrons with scents and vapours, waxes and concoctions. The Yemenite policeman asks me if I can teach his children English. The Austrian librarian comes to see me, and tells me she is of a nervous disposition. She had her jaw broken last year by someone who couldn't find the book he wanted. My playing un-nerves her. So I go to the municipality, a long pale building, with grey shuttered windows. A secretary on the third floor laughs at me, but gives me the phone numbers of three headmasters. But she thinks they will find my request odd. At the hospital, they tell me to bring my instrument to work and entertain the patients. Then they all laugh.

§

One morning at five o'clock the peace of the neighbourhood is broken by trucks rumbling into our square to deposit more building materials on the dead grass. Then men with electric drills arrive and begin to attack the ground. They put up a notice in Hebrew. Before I take Danny to Marta I run back home to check the word in a dictionary. Miklat. What a mental block that was. They are building an air-raid shelter.

Miklat was one of the first words I learned here. Now I lead my son past the noisy drilling as dust clouds around us. My boy puts his hands to his ears and says "Br-r-r-r-r-r!" I say "Br-r-r-r-r-r" too. Marta meets us at the gate. She shouts that while they drill the foundations of the shelter, she will keep the children inside because of the noise and dust.

But next morning Danny doesn't cover his ears. He trots along beside me, eager, and curious. He calls "Shalom" to the men working, so I look at them. Arabs. Three men and a boy who can't be more than seventeen. The young one calls out "Shalom," and waves at Danny.

They are almost certainly from Gaza, which is half an hour away. They are employed in building an air-raid shelter which will be used in the next war that we and they will fight. War is the topic I have avoided since I got here. Influenced by righteous friends in London (and righteous myself) I avoid wars. I won't need to go into the army here for a while, and when I do go, it will be as doctor, not combatant. I give lifts to soldiers sometimes and they practise their English on me. I try out my Hebrew on them. The news here is always about conflict, of course, but I turn the sound down until Kojak or The Rockford Files. A war against crime in America seems as far from me here as it did in London. This conflict between Israel and the Arabs has nothing to do with me.

§

I object to violence, hatred, persecution. I object to slogans, jargon, extreme nationalism. I object to the newspapers of the world and to the headlines they flash before me. Paradings of rights and wrongs, half-rights, half-wrongs, in multitudinous disguises. Sometimes I long for the London days, when we sat outside the pub in summer and drank lager, or under seventeenth century copper kettles on antique benches in the winter – and discussed (leaving out Ireland because it was too close) all the places in the world where violence held sway.

I don't object to my son, even when he wriggles and screams while having his hair washed. His screams truly have innocence and purity in them. Very occasionally he decides to have a temper tantrum. For reasons we rarely understand, and fortunately not often, he will let rip, rending the air purple with furious howling. It's not easy, being three and a half, and having recently been landed with a baby sister.

Daily now, Dan and I watch the walls of the shelter take shape. They sink into the earth rather than rise above it. Iron rods line the walls. A thick roof takes a while to put on. Chimneys rise above the low building, fairy-tale chimneys. I am waiting for the day he asks me, who lives in that house Daddy?

Incurably sociable, he has started chatting to the youngest of the workmen, the Arab boy who works with the older men on the shelter. What's your name he asks in Hebrew and the youth answers in a gentle voice, "Sami." He bends down to say it, and when he bends his body is young and delicate.

One morning, at ten minutes to eight Danny stops by the shelter and invites Sami to tea. That is, he reaches up a small hand, and pulls Sami along with us. Sami follows, grinning. I have noticed he often looks bored with and resentful of the work he has to do. I have put it down to natural resentment against an occupying colonial force (me) and nothing more. But now I realise he isn't cut out for it at all. His slim figure looks weak, his hands narrow and clean. He beams with delight at the invitation my son has extended and the two of them walk ahead of me towards the gan.

A word about my son's education. When the children are not playing inside, in the poorly decorated villa which is Marta's home, they are out in the garden giving tea parties. Not sure what they call them in Hebrew, but we call them tea parties. Marta possesses dozens of old plastic yoghourt containers. A few genuine children's tea services – all in plastic, and endless supplies of sand, gravel, leafy mud for cakes, and occasionally, as a real treat, inch-high jugs of water. Marta stands back, blinking in the sun, as Danny settles Sami on top of a blue tyre, then hands him an inch-high teacup. Sami pretends to sip at it then slides off the tyre.

"Tea party at eight in the morning!" Marta says. I am embarrassed. This woman who survived concentration camps is entrusted by me to educate our toddler, and he invites a Palestinian Arab to have tea with him, and very early in the morning.

"Danny," she says cheerfully, "Your friend has work to do, and I have a gan to run. Let him finish his tea, and say goodbye for now!" But she smiles at the young man, who smiles back at her. Both of them gaze for a second at my happy son. Then Sami and I leave together. To be frank, he doesn't look as though the annihilation of the State of Israel is his main aim in life. But surely he must - if he gives it any thought - wish I had stayed in London.

§

Afternoon. Summer. Four o'clock. The baby wakes from her nap. My wife wipes over the kitchen floor with a damp cloth soaked in bleach and the white tiles are cooled, and cool our feet, giving off a fresh smell against the dry gusts that blow through when the shutters are open. Danny is in our tiny garden playing with a stick and an understandably apprehensive beetle. I hear his excited voice.

"Imma! Abba! They are here. My friends have come!"

Out in the garden he hops onto the low wall. To one side stands Sami, reserved, holding a packet of sweets. Approaching from the road, I see Marta, looking weary in spite of her siesta. She leans heavily against the wall. The only seating we have apart from the disintegrating wall is a straw rocking chair, sun-blanched and shriveled.

"Please come . . . in," I say to both of them. But I hear my own voice, sounding doubtful. What am I doubting?

"We were invited by Danny, and we must sit where he wants us!" said Marta. "I think he wants us out here." The child nods wisely, biting his lip in excitement.

"All right," I agree. "I'll bring drinks out here. Something cold for both of you?"

My innocent child beams from head to toe. Who does he think he is, I whisper to my wife in the kitchen. But she is half asleep and needs to feed the baby. She puts grapefruit juice - in Hebrew, mitz eshkoliot - in four glasses, placing them on a fibre glass tray which was a wedding present back in England.

Both Marta and Sami have fallen in love with Danny. Their delight in him shows. But me? I'm imagining telling someone back home - I mean back in London. Marta, my son's gannenet and Sami, his friend who builds air-raid shelters, came for after-noon tea in the garden. My mind dances round the situation. Sami is a Palestinian and is employed by an Israeli builder to erect a shelter which will protect us during the next war.

"You don't look as though building is your regular job," Marta says fearlessly to the young man.

"No. I work with my uncles. They are from Gaza."

There is a corner, a place where the road out of Ashkelon meets the main road that runs to Gaza. There is an open-air display of cane furniture from there; sellers wait for Israelis to stop their cars, get out and buy it. I don't know a great deal about life in Gaza. Three times since we came here I have gone with other medics and held clinics. Mother and Baby. Children. Adults. Never enough time, and not enough equipment. Made me feel uneasy.

"And where are you from?" Marta asks Sami in Hebrew.

"Jaffa," says the young man, "Yaffo." And my understanding of Israeli demographics adjusts a little. Of course, there are lots of people like Sami. Arabs who stayed in the country when the War of Independence happened. Almost a million people. "But I will soon be moving to Ashkelon." He looks at me. So he knows who I am and where I work, "I will be a nurse at Ashkelon hospital."

And suddenly I'm on a different planet again, and things look different again, and if it's the plight of the Palestinians I've been worried about, then at least I don't need to worry about Sami. Or not too much. A few months from now and we'll be working together. The hospital is a ten-minute walk away.

"It's a good hospital," Marta assures Sami, "though they haven't done much for my cystitis! But when I broke my leg last year, they fixed it."

"Glad to hear it," he replies.

Danny offers us refreshments. A plastic plate which he holds at a precarious angle has broken biscuits and crisps about to slide onto the grass.

"Oppah!" says Sami, in perfect Hebrew, which means "watch out" or "be careful," and moves like lightning to catch the plate. One biscuit tumbles but the others are saved.

"So you'll live at the hospital?" I ask. I have walked past a building which is the Nurses Home. I'd assumed the nurses were all women, but on reflection that is old-fashioned. It is nineteen seventy-nine, women can be doctors and men can be nurses.

"While I am training, yes. After that, who knows where I will go."

"You don't need to go anywhere," Danny pipes up. "You can live here. You have built your house here. It's nearly finished!" He points to the shelter, with its row of four steel chimneys, for air to get in and out.

"Oy!" Marta melts with warmth. She bends down and scoops up the child, holding him tight against her, hugging him until his cheeks are red, his eyes drowsy with affection; he falls out of her arms like a squeezed beanbag. "Motek!" She murmurs. Sweet child.

Over the next few weeks Danny learns to go to gan on his own. One of us stands at the gate to watch him negotiate a way across the small square, and we hear the click of her gate as Marta, a shadow in the sunny distance, lets him in to her little kingdom.

It's been a while since Sami has worked on the shelter, which is close to completion. My wife and I think we are unlikely to see him again. That is, I'll come across him when he starts his training at my hospital. But socially? Probably not.

One evening, a rare evening, Danny is at a little friend's house, and we go for a stroll, taking the baby in her new buggy, walking amongst eucalyptus trees down the narrow pathways of Afridar, our neighbourhood. The streets of Ashkelon. As usual, I complain about not having anywhere to play my saxophone, but get scant sympathy from my wife, who says she has given up everything to look after our children, and I should stop grumbling. Then, as we pass Marta's house and the gan, I am astonished to see her coming out of it with Sami, who holds a notebook and a clipboard.

"My teacher!" he says to us.

"Sami wanted Hebrew lessons," she says.

"The best! A wonderful teacher," he declares.

"Your Hebrew seems fine to me," I say. But my Hebrew is still inadequate so I can't judge that of others.

"It is reasonably good," he agrees, "but I want it to be better."

"Of course you do," says Marta. "And after that, I'll send him to you, because he'll need better English in due course."

My mind jumps ahead of me. I see Sami a few years from now, a highly qualified nurse or maybe by then a doctor, and his Hebrew and Arabic are both perfect but he might want to travel, who knows maybe to London.

"My wife is going to start teaching English lessons soon," I say hopefully, though I know that's not the main thing she wants out of her life. We leave it at that.

§

Some time later I collect a sleepy looking Danny from the gan. As we pass the miklat we realise something has changed. The mess has been cleared. No wheelbarrows, and the skip has gone.

"It's finished, now," I say to him, optimistically. He shakes his little hands, his gesture for enjoyment, pleasure.

"Sami's house! Now he'll come and live in it."

"Sorry darling, but no; It isn't Sami's house." One of those moments. His little face screws up in fury, he stamps his feet, waves his arms, and starts to scream.

"Yes it is it is it is. I did watch him build it. He did build it for a house!"

What has happened to my son's English, and what is it he understands about this shelter that I have failed to tell him? I stand helplessly alongside my near-hysterical boy. His sobs seem to last hours. He must be tired, needs to sleep. No afternoon nap today. Eventually, he relents and allows me to pick him up and hold him, as he slowly calms down, and his beautiful head flops despairingly on my shoulder.

§

The saxophone. What am I to do. The calm psychologist comes to see me, suggests I have a problem, offers me a Gestalt therapist further up the coast in Ashdod. She lives in a wheelchair but has overcome disability and leads a joyous life. I explain that I don't want a psychologist thank you I just need somewhere to play my saxophone.

Danny shoots up a temperature, and we agree this is why he lost his cool earlier, over such a silly matter. Surely he must have known that the now permanently locked concrete shelter between us and Marta's gan is nothing like anyone's home.

Later I have a dream. I approach the miklat, and the padlock is open, the door moves freely, and with a few light steps there I am, inside it. It's a round white dome above and around me, tinted with shades of pale pink. Joyously, free at last, I close the door tight, and start to play. My mouth grips the cool mouthpiece of my instrument with as much passion as I have ever felt, and my fingers turn to music with reckless energy. The notes rise and fall. I play an air-raid siren, pause to breathe, laugh out loud. I syncopate, improvise, stop for breath, then off I go again, making music to heal the world.

The Saint on the Wall

The saint on the wall says sh-sh. His halo dull behind the glass, his expression of enigmatic repose curtained by sunbeams and dust. The pallor of his skin. Sh-sh. One long white finger to his lips.

Spotty Sandra, her tie crooked, sits on a mahogany chair ignoring the saint on the wall. Theorems tabled in front of her, she puzzles over geometry. Then Rosalind Lee enters. She makes critically for Sandra's tie – to straighten it. Her large pink knuckles blur the polar coordinates.

Young Pixie bobs in, her long wavy hair floating behind her. Curtsies, laughs, throws the Authorised Daily Prayer Book of Synagogues down on the heavy reading table. Her mother's left-over pink-and-blue flowered wallpaper glows from its covers. The saint on the wall presumes silence.

The three Littman girls come in. Their faces composed in fixed ratios – as the ratio of their status is fixed. The others come to attention, open their books.

"What will we do today then?" Pixie asks. In the pause before a reply a hushed rumble rises beneath the library. The noise of the feet of seven hundred girls in the big hall, as they stand up to greet their Miss Martin. But up here in the library prayers are of a different texture. And the saint on the wall keeps guard, one long white finger to his lips.

Dark-eyed Sandra and her blue-eyed fair-haired cousin Pixie, Rosalind Lee and The Littmans - Susan the first Littman, Becky the second Littman, and Vivien the little Littman. One two three four five six. The saint on the wall says sh-sh.

Resting their dark-green uniformed thighs against the mahogany, they open their books. The seven hundred in the hall, through the art room and down the stairs, raise their voices in a hymn. Prayers for the six up here in the library rise up to the saint on the wall, who keeps a serene finger at his lips, motioning quiet.

They all read. They make mental sounds in their heads of the ancient black letters, going from right to left on their pages. While reading, Sandra whispers to Susan Littman: "Have you heard what Rosalind did on Saturday night?"

Becky watches their whispering. Susan Littman, pale with the effort of understanding the page, waits to hear. Turning back to encounter several more black squiggles, contorted and cut, arranged in prone oblongs, Sandra, embarrassed today by her acne, informs, "She was in the airing cupboard with Andrew – and she took her bra off." Susan Littman freezes in the sun.

"How do you know?"

Sandra confirms, her eyes sliding back to the ordered troops on her page. "First she told me. Then he told me."

Susan Littman forgets to concentrate. Following with her eyes the black wrought-iron signs which translated mean "who has chosen us from all nations and given us your law," Susan Littman wonders things. One: what was the shape and nature of Rosalind Lee`s breasts? Or was it one half of the bra only? Did she actually take it off? Or did he? Was it hot and stifling in the airing-cupboard? Could they breathe? What had Andy said to her? She was certainly sylphlike, wasn't she?

Susan Littman now whispers to Becky Littman who moves through her letters on the page the way a train moves through a dark tunnel. "Ros took her bra off in the airing cupboard with Andy. The bitch." Becky blushes and laughs out loud. The saint on the wall says sh-sh.

"Well, what do we say now?" Pixie demands guidance from the Littmans because the Littmans can best negotiate a path through the labyrinth of lines and letters.

"The next prayer," says Susan Littman with determination, aiming for no less than God, "will be on page eleven." Downstairs seven hundred turn to page twenty-nine for the Lord's Prayer, before the second hymn. The saint on the wall says sh-sh.

"I don't know how anyone could do a thing like that." Little Vivien Littman shudders and promises herself she never will.

Becky Littman begins to do sums. Her mind travels along the spiritual railway lines in front of her. Kept straight by the layout, the square forward-chugging movement of the black carriages along which her eye roves. It would be wrong to read the English, printed coldly, with thees and thous, on the opposite page. So this comfortable journey through signs is wholesome, reassuring; and meanwhile she can do sums.

Equations. Andy plus Rosalind Lee. Though obviously he can't really care for her. How could he love someone who voluntarily took her bra off in the airing cupboard? How did it smell in there? Was it hot?

What did Andy say to her? Slender or not, he had kissed her, Becky, once before all the others. There had been a sensation of long damp pressure, and a touch of grains of sand on his lips. A surging repulsion that some of his saliva might now be on her lips. However dry his lips felt – and they didn't feel dry. No excitement. Her hands by her sides, then on his back, so the wind blew them into white stone. Till the bus came. Nothing much. Except the knowledge that Susan Littman had taken the earlier bus home and was crying in bed while Andy pressed saliva and sand against Becky's closed mouth. But the inner excitement arising all the same, especially on thinking it over and telling Susan – later.

Becky Littman watches black letters. Square, rigid, they melt under her abstract gaze, grow tiny feet, tramp off over the pale page which humps up and turns solid, a fawn mountain which is Rosalind Lee's breasts exposed to Andy in the airing cupboard. Were there other clothes there, drying? Neatly folded in the dark? What did they say to each other?

It is time for clear thinking. Becky Littman calculates now that Andy is lost to her. First there is Susan, paler than ever, praying with new intensity, moved to stand a little away. Her eyes almost frantic, scratching for meaning on the printed page. Andy put his tongue in her mouth. And if Susan doesn't in the end get Andy, or he her – well, then there is always Slender Rosalind waiting. Now that she has taken her bra off. If you`ve done it once, are you likely to do it again? And that is not to forget Pixie, with her fair hair and apparent innocence. Lolita was written about someone like Pixie, wasn't it?

The saint on the wall says Sh-sh. It being the last day of the term, the seven hundred sing "Lord Dismiss us with Thy Blessing."

Sadly, Sandra crouches over her solid geometry again. Something she has neglected to do. Becky Littman watches her, the tears that come into her eyes, trickle down, plop into Euclid's magic circles. Sometimes Becky pities Sandra. By virtue of having a mild case of acne, she is less likely than the others to have a chance of attracting Andy. But she is unpredictable. Sometimes, you never know when, her skin clears for a few days, and she beams on the world, prancing at a party from one mirror to another.

"If I was any good at geometry I'd offer to help," Becky lies sweetly. The saint on the wall says sh-sh.

"What do we say now?" urges Pixie petulantly.

So. Andy is allocated to Susan, or to Rosalind, thinks Becky, and Sandra seems happy to spend time with that other boy, Peter, who smells of egg sandwiches, so let her have him. But then – who will be left? Who do I want to love? Is there anyone around I might be in love with, asks Becky in panic. The saint on the wall expects decorum. Who will I love, Becky wonders again.

Do Pixie and her best friend Karen from the other school count, wonders Becky. Being only thirteen? Oh let them stay thirteen. Meanwhile, then they can have Clive and Derek. Clive and Derek will do perfectly for them because they are too young. Let them all stay young!

There is . . . the Viennese boy from the other side of town. But his parents took him to live on the wrong side of town for a purpose. They never wanted him to belong, did they? You would think, Becky knew this to be true, that after Hitler they would have learned something. But there you are, people don't learn. So he doesn't count. Curls or no curls.

And that – leaves Frankie Priceman. With the party season approaching. Goodwill. Who will I feel goodwill towards, asks Becky. The saint on the wall says sh-sh . . .

Which leaves, muses Becky, having done the whole calculation again, Frankie Priceman for me. Frankie Priceman having previously been ignored by all the others, apart from the outspoken American girl Serena Weinberg who flew in and out of the very small community in a heatwave last summer. Serena had cradled him for one hot evening on the sofa in the Littman's lounge, and his young prickly beard gave her a rash all over her wild west cheeks.

"Look what he did to my face!" She rubbed it, making Becky laugh. Then she turned to her sixteen-year old not-quite-lothario, "Never mind, Frank. I forgive you. If not in this life – then in the next!" Becky had never heard anything like this.

"Serena's second step grandmother," Frankie Priceman declared not rudely at all to the whole room, "was related to the poet Conrad Aiken. Isn't that something? Myself, I prefer Eliot. We shall not cease from exploration, and the end of all our exploring will be to arrive where we started and know the place for the first time."

Serena returned to America a month later.

Sandra draws a careful line under her last problem. The voices from the hall crescendo. Frankie Priceman's aggressive face presents itself to Becky through the last lines of the penultimate prayer selected by her big sister. Hear O Israel.

Susan Littman's eyes glow like searchlights over the words. Her stare prises them open, as if they are ancient treasure left for her alone to discover. Becky thinks, watching – she has the words, and Andy. The voices in the hall begin the descent towards the final note. Soon Miss Arden-Keen will start the incidental music. Flocks in Pastures Safely Grazing. The seven hundred will leave the hall.

Frankie Priceman's expression is not inviting. He vaults with Becky's eyes from word to word, each group of letters a bed of nails on which his bodiless head rests, glaring at her. No waterfalls of emotion and loving-kindness gush from his eyes.

Well, what if Frankie Priceman isn't really what I imagine who I might love? Becky closes her book, attentive to an inner feeling that squirms, stirs, rustles. There is actually something unusual about him. So it follows that what I feel for him could well be a bit unusual as well. Strange, frightening, and very unusual. Who knows? Who knows what will be, and spotty Sandra can't be as clever as she thinks she is.

Feet turn out of the big hall. Seven hundred Oxford lace-ups drum up the stairs. Soon the six will leave the library and be submerged. The thunder of the feet getting louder. See you tomorrow, say the six. . .

After the library empties, chairs creak in anticipation of ankles winding round their legs, green skirts trailing. The tables shine. The saint on the wall views his empty hermitage with glass eyes. Sunlight streams in, into the silence. Flooded in quiet, the saint on the wall keeps one lone white finger to his thin lips.

Seventh Floor

We're in a hotel room on the seventh floor with a sea view. But the sea view is at the wrong angle.

"I've been hoping," you say, "that I would be able to see the sea from my bed, when I go to sleep. And when I wake up."

Such is your frail state of health and my alertness to it that when you say go to sleep my mind says die and when you say wake up my inner voice says miracle. Five Stars should have been Three Stars. I phone Reception three times, and finally they bring more pillows. You need two extra for your head and shoulders, and one to go under your legs. We're not sure if the pain that shoots from your calves through your knees is wear and tear of ninety-two-year-old joints, or something to do with veins. You got varicose veins when I was born. You never wanted surgery. "I'll wear elastic stockings for the rest of my life if I have to."

We're here because the frustration of living with your carer who only speaks Tagalog finally got to you. You gave her a five-day holiday, and announced excitedly on the phone: "You're coming to see me anyway aren't you? You can come with me to the hotel. I need a holiday from Maria!"

Slowly you prepare for bed. I know that I started life in very close proximity to you, but that was sixty-four years ago. I don't know what I need to do for you. I don't know how much I want to do. I want you to settle down to sleep easily. I suggest calling Reception again to ask them if they can move the beds around so we can position you with a view of the sea as you go to sleep.

"Don't do that. They won't want to move the beds."

§

Taking a last look at the sea, you note a crowd of youngsters making bonfires on the beach. The sun has half set. The sea is greys, and dying blues. I want to tell you about a Wallace Stevens poem. In that November in Tehuantepec. He describes the sea, over and over. A poem rich in colour words. But the poems you love are a certain few. Mostly they rhyme. Mostly they are pre-Wallace Stevens. All our differences are irrelevant now. I am close to you. But I don't come as close as you need. You lie on your pillow. You laugh with me, as we share critical notes on the baked aubergine we ate downstairs. A pregnant waitress for whom we both should have felt compassion. But didn't. You say, lightly, "It's a shame Doug didn't come with you this time."

"Next time," I reassure you. Then something makes me say, brightly, in order to emphasize the ordinariness of everything, to make it clear this is not an evening when someone might be about to die,

"I think I might just pop downstairs to the lobby. Perhaps see if the others are there."

"No," you say urgently, "Please stay until I'm asleep." I might have moved my head, or blinked, or given some sign, "Why don't you just sit on the balcony, and look at the sea?"

§

I'm twenty-four. It's the third day of my honey-moon. We're an odd couple in some ways. Made for each other in others. I know he doesn't love me. That is to say, he's told me a hundred times that he does, but he will admit, fifteen years hence that what drew him into life with me wasn't love. Not the way other people experience it. It was that sense - and I have it too (I do love him) - a sense that we could learn to live well together. I started to love him in broad daylight. We were walking in Yorkshire, and we came to a wrought-iron gate which was locked. The grass-flecked gravel path went on regardless, but we were held back by the locked gate. We stood still, not bothered. Daffodils, I recall. Rain and daffodils, and something about his mouth, as I glanced sideways, and a little upwards, his mouth against the clouds, patches of blue sky showing round them.

Fifteen years hence, fifteen years from to-night, when he has learned to love me, I will have stopped loving him. Our marriage will be flimsy for a while. Flimsy as a spider's web.

Tonight, we're on the little veranda of our hotel. He lights a cigarette, and we talk. He tells me things about his parents. Then we both yawn, and for the first time in two days and two nights I feel an urge to go to sleep. To go to bed to sleep. I'm so tired my head spins.

I turn my head to look at the sky, cloudless, summery, Mediterranean. Black. And against the black, the stars. Hundreds and thousands of them. There was nothing in the brochure. And as I gaze, dizzily, I move, I float, I drift away from him, until I'm out there spinning. Out there. He says, and I nod, "Let's go to bed."

I'm back in the room, having closed the heavy sliding door so no one can squeeze through it. You smile. You think you've been watching the sea through me, but that is not the case. I was re-membering my honeymoon. When the fear of being high on a balcony first got me, round the ankles. A fear so powerful, it is like a deranged creature prowling, advancing, pouncing. It can reach out with tentacles, limbs of pure muscle. It can pull, or push a helpless person over the edge. Any edge. Part-icularly a high one.

These days, what happens round my ankles, and a few inches up each calf is this. Eczema. Eczema of the kind that people in their sixties get. No known cause. Likely to become chronic. It's worst at the front. An assortment of different shapes in red, some raised, some not. All itchy. Unbelievably, incurably, intrepidly, itching. I beam at you, by way of greeting, try to let the impact of an outgoing daughterly smile muffle the itching. Snuff it out. Cool it. Kill it. Stop it.

You relax, anyway, and lie back, warm-hearted mother. Though in a few seconds your rosy round face crumples, turns into the death mask of a dying old woman. I either want you to die, quickly, effortlessly, now, while I'm here. Or I want you to fall asleep, and sleep through the night. Your mouth opens. You begin to snore. Head back, mouth wide open. Is this what I'll look like dead or dying? I can't imagine being ninety-two, myself. I can't imagine getting there, being there, then dying. I'm absolutely not supposed to scratch. I've smeared creams on, and will put more on later.

I can't sleep. It's more than just the itching. It's the fact that I know you'll wake me several times. When you get up in the night you won't take your stick, as you stumble past my bed. I'll wake, then, jittery. I'll grab my legs, start to scrape the skin with my nails, then remember the creams. As I get out of bed, I'll see you making your way too. Perhaps you'll reach out, clutch my arm, for support.

At school, when I was ten, the girl who sat next to me, Tina Hope, had eczema too. Eczema of childhood. I have it of late middle age. You've been spared eczema on your legs. But you've had plenty other things to deal with. Sometimes I list them. Sometimes you do. I was ten when you had your first operation, and Miss West sent me home from school with a huge bouquet of flowers. The nurses laughed out loud when I was guided into your room with flowers. That little face, surrounded by chrysanthemums, they marveled. For years I associated operations not with illness, or fear. Certainly not with death. I associated them with flowers, and me smiling at people smiling back.

Miss West, you remember, was the teacher who had us polishing our desks, and the little brass inkwells. Every Friday we took in dusters, wood polish, and Brasso. I loved Fridays for this reason. The dark oak of the desk reminded me of the brisket you used to give us. Although I hated the fat, and the gristle. The wood, like the dark meat, had cracks running through it, and looked nourishing. But Tina Hope must have suffered agonies. She would turn her hand like a fluttering wing of some living creature, something caged and trying to escape. I imagine cool air on the skin helped for a second or two.

Another thought. You might, as you walk unevenly past my bed, trip on the corner of the sheet, or hit the side of that low piece of furniture I only ever see in hotel rooms. Long, low, not quite a sideboard, because not enough cupboards. Or it'll happen in the bathroom. You'll get to the toilet, for the mixed discomfort and relief of passing water and faeces. You'll lean forward, head close to your knees. As you get up, after you've washed your hands - you still fear infections – you'll turn too quickly, sway, clutch at the transparent bathroom wall, then slip in a faint on the floor. Your thud and cry will be a beat and a wail in an orchestrated symphony of dying sounds. I know what that will sound like because I hear it in my head as I try, unsuccessfully to fall asleep myself.

Suddenly you snort, cough, jerk, breath in sharply, cough roughly. You open your eyes to see where I am. I am sitting up. You smile warmly, lovingly, gently. We've done it. Mother and Daughter. Between us we've mapped a way through. We selected enough of the right paths, though there were sometimes alarming numbers of wrong ones to avoid.

"Leave the windows open," you insist. How can I say no? "I love the sound of the sea."

Shakily I get up, and drag open the heavy sliding doors. We are seven storeys up. Glancing down, I feel the fizz of vertigo, and the backs of my legs tremble. The sea is darker now. I can't see surfers anymore, but hear their high cries, their whoops. Behind them, beyond us, the rich background is of rushing water and distant thunder. The waves rise up to find me, like wet limbs of pure muscle, pulling and pushing.

Waving in the Wind

Heather was twenty-three, and not long married when she heard voices in the garden one night. It seemed, she thought, that they came from the hawthorn tree, or the ash tree, and sometimes from behind the splendid magnolia, which broke her heart in the spring by blossoming only days before the march winds began to blow. A few hours of cruel breezes and the delicate petals floated helplessly to the ground.

But after a few months, and a change of seasons, she stopped imagining that trees could talk. She put the voices down to the heightened sense of everything that seemed to engulf her as a result of falling in love and getting married.

One night, Rod stood beside her as they looked out at their garden, which was long and full of old trees. Rod suggested that there might be people (possibly a couple whose families forbade them to meet), who sheltered in what they called fondly "our Arboretum," meeting in secret, murmuring sweet nothings, occasionally breaking into passionate moans, which was why Heather had to open the window and shout at them to be quiet. After shouting, she would lean into the darkness, and see no one.

"Perhaps," Heather suggested, "they heard us and ran away! Or perhaps trees do have souls!"

§

She was seventy, as was Rod when they decided to leave the large house in Amersham and move right into London town. Rod was retiring from his work as an architect.

Heather was sorry to retire. For years she had taught English as a Foreign Language in Watford. Saying goodbye to her last class of students made her cry. Mrs Haq the doctor's wife, Calin the computer engineer from Bucharest, Sudanese actor Hameis, her favourite students, brought her a bejewelled black elephant from the Oxfam shop as a farewell gift.

They all wrote on a card, its cover saying Thank You in thirty-nine languages. "Without you our new lives in England would have been so much harder!"

And now Rod and Heather were to have new lives of their own with a real London postcode. They first viewed the flat, Eleven Forest Court, on a December afternoon. They hardly noticed the shrubs and trees outside, in the space between the new-build block and the tube line.

New-built and sophisticated. Second floor. Lift, underground garage, walk-in showers, lights in the ceiling and underfloor heating. A miracle of engineering and architecture, everyone said, and best thing of all? The station, its track parallel with the side of the building. Yards away.

Parkside Wood Tube Station

A park at the edge of a wood? Or a wood beside a park? That first December day they saw neither park nor wood. Looking out of the wide windows they saw the bridge, joining the two sides of the line. Through the double glazing they heard the trains, starting or slowing, nothing high speed, coming in and out of the station.

Our very own station, they told everyone. We love the sound of the trains, they said, and meant it. The children congratulated their parents on the skill of the downsizing. What could be better? This new-build of seventeen flats, fronted by a lawn, with low laurels and a wall for toddlers to climb over. Forest Court.

A Chinese family lived on the first floor. Their veranda distinguished them from the rest of the flats from the outset. Their child wore pink bonnets and white shoes, her glossy black hair hanging in a fringe over her cute face. Heather put plant-pots and a tub on her small veranda, but the Chinese veranda was filled from the outset with tubs of herbs. You could feel the healing in the air, just by walking past. The grandmother played the piano elegantly. Chopin, and Schubert "impromptus."

There was an electric gate. When a car nosed up to it, it opened automatically. One day the Chinese grandmother set out for the gate, her reserved-looking husband beside her, and collapsed. She fell on the ground, just where a car would be, except they weren't a car, they were people, one about to die. Heather watched from her veranda, as the woman lay in a crumpled heap, and the man shouted for help, shaking jerkily.

Each flatholder had been given an electronic key fob. You were supposed to hold the key towards the gate, press a grey button, and hey presto, the gate slid open. Except on this occasion, with someone dying on the ground in front of it the gate wouldn't open. So Heather (Rod was at The National Gallery) dialed nine nine nine. Now the grandfather knelt beside his wife, crying out, waving his arms. It was windy. Above them it was for a moment as if the ash, sycamore, the giant horse chestnut were alive. Their branches gesticulated frantically. Witnesses.

Ambulance men tried to scale the side gate, but that wouldn't open either, so one of them took a hammer, and opened it with a clanging so loud that the sound sliced through Heather's head, axe-sharp. After the clangs came an aftersound, like a human voice but sharper, more desperate. Her brain felt bruised. Though Rod suggested later that however traumatic the event had seemed to the onlooker, it probably only took moments for the gate to be opened.

"Relax," he said.

"Don't tell me to relax." She looked more stressed than he had seen in years. "If the gate had been opened a few minutes earlier? Might they have revived the poor woman?"

Living in Forest Court was like living in a small village. There was a council, and a Board of

Directors. The Chair of the Board was called James Steel. He was an engineer who had been a builder. Three months after the tragic death, there was a meeting of all the members of the village. They met in a pub called The Apple Tree. Heather addressed James Steel.

"How we can be expected to live, "she asked urgently, "in a place where we can't control our own front door!" He explained carefully that the outer gate was not anyone's individual front door. The mechanism was complex, so he and only he must be the keeper of the emergency code. He was an engineer, he understood metals, locks, keys and their codes.

From then on, that clang, metal on metal kept echoing in Heather's head. Sometimes it was so loud, she had to hold her ears. Rod comforted her. Don't worry. We're all shocked and upset, we wouldn't be normal if we weren't.

But it happened again, and kept happening, that Heather would be woken by the loud metallic sound, even as the nights got shorter, the days longer, and it was spring, then late spring, and even as the sun shone more and more so that most of the village folk, the village of Forest Court, got on with their lives, and paid no more attention to the question of the iron gate.

In May, she had a dream. She was in a wood picking bluebells when a branch fell from a tree above her and hit her head. She woke with a jump, trembling.

Everyone said moving house at seventy was the second most stressful thing you could experience.

The first was a bereavement. But they did try to concentrate on the fun, the stimulation of their new lives. Two or more mornings a week Heather would be up early, leaving Forest Court (through the side gate), climbing the twenty-six steps of the bridge, then down twenty-four on the other side of the track, through the automated ticket machine with her Freedom Pass, and onto the platform to wait for a train to take her to town.

In London Town she became adventurous as the weather improved. She went to Art Galleries, book-shops, parks and theatres, and came home cult-urally enriched. This was a city like no other. It had a history of a thousand years and was the home of every great invention in the world! (An usher at the National told her this, at a matinee of a play set in nineteen twenty-seven.)

In June she encountered James Steel on the station platform. He stepped cheerfully off the train she was about to board. He was a short, stocky man, with thick grey hair and a rectangular face. He wore rimless glasses. He beamed jovially at Heather, and spoke with bonhomie and a kind of pride.

"Our railway system is the oldest in the world," he enthused. "Did you know?"

"No."

"It started way back in the sixteenth century. Old wagonways on wooden rails, that's what they had, here. Do you like living in London?"

"Yes thank you."

"Flat comfortable? Do the trains disturb you?"

"Yes thank you. No. We love them."

Then he pointed to the gap between the train track and Forest Court, to the mass of trees and shrubs that were flourishing this summer, ash, oak, sycamore, privet, a veritable natural arbour in a wood made of stone and steel . . .

"We need to keep an eye on these," he said, narrowing his eyes, surveying the urban oasis.

"I like the trees."

"Give them half a chance," he warned, "they'd overrun us. It would take them a decade or so to overwhelm Forest Court, but they could damage the train tracks in months. In fact," he peered at the branches above their heads, the leaves blowing innocently in the breeze, "they need cutting back. I'll call Transport for London in the morning."

Heather felt the blood rush to her face, and her heart began to pound. She felt suddenly protective towards these innocent trees and shrubs, caught as they were between the rail track and Forest Court.

She nodded a polite goodbye and turned to get on the train. She sat down as the doors closed. The train moved off with a hum and a clicking sound. She looked at her fellow-passengers, their shoes, their bags, their faces. A couple stood protectively over their baby, secure in a buggy, its tiny face staring up at the collection of people, bright little eyes moving back and forth, watching, watching.

A homeless man came through the carriage, thin, pale, bald, wearing a tattered denim jacket, sleeves in shreds. She pulled out her purse and handed him a ten pound note. Thank you, bless you, he sounded stunned, and everyone looked away. For a moment neither she nor the homeless man existed at all.

By July Heather was beginning to wonder, in the moments of distraction that come as you fall asleep or wake up, whether they might have made a mistake. Moving to London at their time of life, from the suburb where the cycle of their lives ran from magnolia to rhododendrons, from rhododendrons to roses and geraniums, then on to dahlias. Heather had particularly loved the smoke bush, which really did look like clouds of purple smoke, and cast cushions of colour over the garden, making every autumn beautiful. Not to mention the crimson berries that decorated the garage wall.

But here, now it was high summer. London in sunshine was four degrees hotter than anywhere in the country. The spaces between the living room window and the tube line were lush with forestry. Branches sprouted where there had been none. On the sloping lawn below the side windows, squirrels frolicked. They sprinted up the horse chestnut tree in seconds, and swung delicately from branch to twig. Flying sprites of nature, joyful in the wind.

In May, blossom had adorned the horse chestnut tree, tiny white flowers, pink at the base, floating gracefully down to cover the grass like confetti. Now, its leaves showed crustiness, browning at the edges, and spiky green conker cases could be seen. Not autumn yet, but it would come. Now, Heather thought, during these summer months, now, if I'm not at peace now, I can never be. She lay in bed, determined to remain calm, and happy. At four in the morning there were birds already chirping. And the night trains, which Transport for London had set going, were no more than the sound of a different sea, gentle through the double glazing, never harsh even when the windows were open....

§

Heather stood on the small slope of grass, which was on the Forest Court side of the wire fence. On the other side was a thicket of shrubbery, with a clump of trees so thick you couldn't actually see the trains that were passing.

She turned to leave Forest Court, pressing the green knob to the right of the small gate, which she then pulled open to let herself through. She looked up at the majestic horse-chestnut, planted a hundred years ago. Under its branches on one side the iron stairway led up to the bridge over the tube line. Paint was peeling off here and there. She climbed the steps with her eyes cast down, witnessing their strength. She thought of the people who had worked here, building this. Fifty, sixty, seventy years ago. Hammering, carrying, perhaps dropping huge slabs of iron and stone. Or was it all done by machines, even then?

She imagined the sound of the men who worked here. No, she heard it. The top of each step was reinforced with a steel covering, on which were impressed rows of letters. Did anyone now wonder what the letters meant, or still mean? Messages, perhaps?

She stood on the bridge, as a father came along, leading a small boy. The child stood, safe between his father's protective body, and the parapet.

"Tains! See tains!" the tot said excitedly.

[Type here]

Heather turned to look back at the stuccoed side of Forest Court, through the windows into her own living room, where moments ago she had been sipping tea. Beneath, below, around, lay a battle-field. Trees, shrubs, grass, squirrels, the odd night fox, mice perhaps, rats certainly. She stood still, like an admiral reviewing his troops. The trees stood tall, so disciplined, so brave, and they would wait, she knew, take their time. Their day would come.

By Madeleine Black

Quarter to six. Here they are. Three of them. A triumvirate of professionals wearing badges. Sweaty Steve, Probation Officer. Svelte Yulia, Case Manager for The Charity. Last but not least, The Psychologist. (I won't name her; she has a stunningly perfect name. I won't falsify that even for the sake of a story!) They are here to introduce me to My Two Volunteers. These, I gather are on their way.

They've been hand-picked for me, my two do-gooders by Svelte Yulia and The Charity. I'm where I was told to be. I'm at a corner table in Patrick`s Place, twenty yards from the tube and Big Issue Seller. I asked for a glass of water. It has a smear on its surface which looks like an oil-slick, except it can't be.

I'm not relaxed. Would anyone expect me to be, less than a month after my release? I'm thirsty but whatever is floating on the water bothers me. Inside, I wouldn't have noticed. I'd have drunk it. Life now is magnified. If I lean to the left the slick disappears. Lean to the right it comes back. Weird.

I'm careful about what things mean. When I was inside, when life had picked me up, swallowed me, spat me out existentially devastated, I kept asking myself why." So what did I do? I began to study

Philosophy. I got one quarter of what could have become a degree. The reason it won't now is because of capitalism and what that does to the chances of people like me. (I read about capitalism as well.)

Before My Volunteers arrive, My Professionals talk me through the rules of our new game. A new script for a film. I often imagine, when someone is talking, that I'm in a film. I'm in half light - dusk, or dawn after a complicated night. I look up and see a camera, and a boomswinger. I love that word.

Synopsis: Ex-offender starts to meet regularly with two women volunteers. The identities of the volunteers to be buried beneath a pile of rules. 1. No surnames. 2. No addresses. 3. All messages to be conveyed through switchboard of The Charity – in other words, no mobile or email contact. Best rule: The Charity will permit them to buy me a meal! Upper budget, Yulia spelled out six pounds. Fish and Chips. Pasta. Bacon Butties.

They are not allowed to ask me what I did. It's up to me whether I tell them or not. The Psychologist suggested I might find it hard to talk about it. This was at our last meeting. The one where we discussed the thirty-page document she had given me to read. "Borderline Personality Disorder." The essence of that was: People are Complicated. Stuff Happens. Nobody knows whether people make stuff happen or whether it happens anyway and the people are fucked, or as she tried silkily to get me to say, why not try using a word like "crushed?" Or any word other than one deliberately calculated to shock?

Here is my take on this world full of lies and distortions. My small contribution to the evil network called humanity is minor, on the scale of things. I committed one accidental crime. One.

§

The volunteers. One looks old enough to be my mother, the other's old enough to be my grand-mother. The aged one has pale grey hair, glasses, and a crushing Christian stare. The younger, one cropped ginger curls, tight to her head. Someone must have coached them before the meeting, because half of it is taken up with a predictable subject. Football. They sit, eyes popping out of their heads, feigning interest. Truth is, I'm pretending too. Part of what the experts call my childhood was that Dad and his step-brother normally came to blows on this topic. They supported different teams. That justified the launch of World War Four every Saturday. Later, I learned the term "collateral damage" and identified myself as that.

By the way - I know from experience that some of the stuff in the novella The Psychologist gave me is crap. For example, the stuff about relationships. It is not true, even if I do have what she called (crossing and uncrossing her legs) a Borderline Personality, that I cannot sustain relationships. OK. I have not sustained All Relationships, but for Christ's sake, who in this world ever has?

This cafe is an odd place. Chunky tables made of thick pale wood. I order pizza and chips, The Professionals share a starter of humus and crudités. Yulia looks embarrassed when she says crudités. I believe she is asking herself does he know this

French word? Mustn't embarrass him! You can see when the food arrives that I am the one living on hostel menus. All my volunteers want is a pot of tea for two. They babble on while I gobble.

§

I was seventeen the day I left what I call, for the sake of brevity, "home." Best day of my life so far. I woke up that morning without the weight of something heavy on my chest. That feeling of dread which always turned out to be justified.

One minute after I left, it was as if I'd never had a home. I spent my cash on a train fare to Windermere, walked a hundred yards and within an hour landed myself a job (waiter), a room, and a god-cousin. All that in a day.

This waitress called Mags befriended me, the way people do in films. She asked me if I'd been baptised. I said no. Her eyes welled up then, and she declared she'd never have grown up OK if it hadn't been for her godparents. So, to launch me in my new life, in which she believed one hundred percent, she pronounced herself my god-cousin. Just like that. It happened. She fancied me, but I didn't fancy her. She had a spotty face and was twenty-four.

My first day off she took me home to meet her dad Cedric, who was as easy-going as she was. Before I returned to Windermere, he'd decided to play the same game. He declared himself my unofficial godfather if I wanted one. I said I did, my eyes blurring.

Three months later, aged eighteen, I moved to Spain. Cedric and Mags gave me a great send-off. Like this time I got my real launch into adult life. "We are your new family!" they kept telling me, as we waved goodbye. We promised to stay in touch and did. They were the sort of people who designed and made their own Christmas cards and sent them weeks in advance but I didn't mind.

I stayed in Spain for five years. I worked in hotels. Oversexed tourists bought me meals - and more. I took a lot of stuff in Spain, and drank too, but I wasn't an addict—not the real thing. Not the way some of my acquaintances were.

Then, in October 1999, the eve of the Millennium I got a letter - people still wrote them - a note from my unofficial godfather Cedric. This letter said two tragic things: he was ill, and Mags was ill. Two different kinds of illness, was how he put it - one physical, one mental. I knew from the fact that he wrote the letter which one of them had physical, which mental. Come and see us, he wrote.

So I ended up back in Windermere, well, just outside. Cedric was half the size I'd remembered from before, he walked with a stick and his skin had gone papery. When I asked him how Mags was he began to cry. This genuinely did my head in.

Somewhere in The Psychologist's document about people like me they go on about vulnerability. Like, people like me can't cope with change and stress. Well, here's the thing. The change and stress with which I proved unable to cope, was not mine. NOT MINE, I repeat. I cope brilliantly with my own change and stress. But. "L'enfer, c'est les autres!"

When Jean Paul Sartre said that, nobody tendered the theory that he had a fucking sorry crushing Borderline Personality.

I went to see Mags in hospital. Recognizing me, she throttled me with a two minute hug, drenching my cheek with tears. I found this revolting. She had the same spots, I think, that she'd had all those years earlier. Red, squeezed, ugly, bruising. She said my name, over and over again, Bob, Bob, Bob, Bob, Bob. Bobby. This made me feel even more alienated. I'd changed it, hadn't I? I changed it in Spain. I'd gone out there as Bob, but after a year became Derek. Anyway, I said, "Doesn't seem too bad here." (Complete lie.) "What do you do with yourself, Mags?"

"Mondays we have a group, Tuesday we go to the park, but I . . . just a minute . . . let me think, Bob. Let me think." She closed her heavy eyes and nodded off. A nurse came in then, woke her up and told her in a loud voice it was time to go to sleep.

I stayed in Cedric's house that night, but I couldn't sleep because he spent the night vomiting noisily. Early in the morning I walked. I took ham from Cedric's fridge, and bread from his breadbin. I took a bottle of water. I never went back there. I never saw either of them again.

I had enough money left for one more night in the small B&B. I decided to stay there and enjoy the scenery because everything about Cedric and Mags had made me feel so sick. And yes, I did take that personally. I took it as what my uncle Duncan called (illustrating it) a punch in the solar plexus. After the crap nonfamily life I'd had, two wholesome people living in the most beautiful place had given me a new identity, only to fall apart themselves, crumble in mind and body and leave me alone again. Anyone human with a heart would have resented this.

§

The B&B was at the bottom of a cul-de-sac down a hill. At the back there was a tumbling brook, like straight out of a film. I got back at seven, it was dark, but the red berries on the shrubs in the garden seemed luminous. The door creaked as I opened it. There was someone there. Sitting on a dilapidated sofa, clutching a handful of maps, tourist guides that she wasn't reading, I saw a vision. That's what it looked like to me. A vision of beauty. Dream come true. Sexy version of Mags minus spots and madness.

"Hello. Didn't know anyone else was staying here. What's your name?"

Freya talked like Kate Middleton. Except she was from Manchester and had masses of blond curls. This made watching her exciting. Sometimes you saw her whole face - gorgeous - sometimes not. She buzzed with something. Buzzed. Absolutely crushing buzzed. If things had gone differently between me and her that night, we would have survived it, and become a couple. We'd met by chance but we knew each other by instinct - and my instincts go deep. We started that evening with the best sex I'd ever had. She sat over me, her hair floating, her body swaying, moaning.

At eight thirty we flaked out on the bed. I sat up when she began pulling stuff out of her green canvas shoulder bag - weed, cannabis, hash. We argued over what to call it. We smoked it. Then the Landlord cracked his knuckles loudly on the door, yelling that he couldn't stand our smell. There was a bit of an altercation. To cut the story short, he most unfairly threw us out.

What did we do? Found a bench on the dark road, and sat on it. For my part I would have chosen to talk about what was going to happen to us, but the nightmare was that she somehow slipped out of my control. Don't ask how. It wasn't anything I did. Just something flipped in her head. She lost it. Or she had hysterical multiple personality disorder, which does exist. She literally became another person. Her hair changed colour in the dark, I think. She started to talk, and kept going. Her voice rose and fell. She was a fox howling in that high-pitched way. Then she was a kitten stuck up a tree.

She'd grown up in Didsbury, wherever that was, an only child, too much attention, with rich parents. I could have wept for her. Her mother sold jewelry in a place called The Royal Exchange. No wonder she reminded me of royalty. Her father ran a business making tee shirts.

"Sounds like you got everything anyone could need!" I said mildly. With this innocent remark of mine, she metamorphosed further, sliding into Hysterical Woman mode.

"Stand up!" she panted, tugging me off the bench, "stand here and let me hit you! I hate them both, I hate everyone, I hate them for giving me so much that I don't know who I am, who I am supposed to be. If I'm alive after the Millennium I'm going to America!" You know, I still held it together, at that point, for both of us. I stood my ground, ignoring the fists pummelling me. Some of the blows left real bruises. No one believed afterwards that they were from a woman. Then I took her hand firmly.

"Come on," I said, "we're going to find a pub. The village is ten minutes away." I led the way. I was mature and patient. Left alone she would have rambled off and been run over. To this day I get nightmares that that happened. I find her lying, head split open, brains on the road. Grey brains and crimson blood.

We came to a pub. It was open, and crowded. I can't give an honest account of what happened next, and no point stopping for a philosophical reverie on the subject which would be titled What is Objective Truth. We met a man. He was taller than me, thinner. He sat in the corner, mournfully.

He looked at Freya, she looked at him, and it started all over again - the flirting, that shaking of her head so the hair came to life, flying, shining. They ended up heads close together, inspecting some minute piece of paper he'd fished out of his pocket. They looked so absorbed, so in their own new world, I felt literally sick. She came over to me, dipped her face to my ear, whispered: I've met this guy. He's a poet!

There was a man sitting opposite me. He bought me drinks. I told him the gist of what had happened. How was I to know he had a personality disorder, too? Probably an impulsive one? At the end of my story, he shuddered, muttering "Bloody Hell!" Next thing I remember – he confronted the poet, told him to leave Freya alone. Then we were dragging him outside, followed by a hysterical Freya.

My memories of the fight are blurred. It happened in a blur of fierce pain. No idea who hit who or hardest, how the injuries were actually inflicted. But I know the poet was killed and I was charged. In my film version, the following happens. The man from the pub, raving, frothing at the mouth, the type of person who invariably attracts trouble, drags the poor poet (bleeding, half-conscious,) and throws him at me like a dummy in a Bond film. I catch him. Or I don't. He falls on the ground, his head hitting a boulder. Sharp intake of breath. I am not entirely to blame. But my crime has happened. In my third prison, I found a book with a poem in it by the poet. Not a good one. Something about fell-walking and death.

Worst thing of all about being what they call rehabilitated is this: I'm not allowed, not by any of them, to talk, certainly not to write about my crime. Verboten. There's a place I go to - for food, a change from the food bank. It's called New World. Guys like me do things like playing scrabble, painting, cooking, yoga. Even writing. But are we allowed to write anything like the truth about anything that happened to us? No we are not.

So here's what I've done. The old volunteer, the one with the glasses, goes to the toilet at least twice during our meetings. Last Tuesday both of them went to the Ladies together, giving each other significant looks. They probably decided to leave their bags on the bench beside me so that I wouldn't think they didn't trust me. One of the bags had a diary sticking out of it. I picked it up, registered the name inside. Then quickly pushed it back. Madeleine Black. This diary belongs to. Blood Group O minus.

So now I'm going to say, just in case any of this, anywhere, anyhow, gets me into trouble, now I declare to the court (you're the court) that this story was written by - wait for it - Madeleine Black. Mrs (she wore a ring) Madeleine Black.

From the Dining Room Table

It is three o'clock on a Shabbat Afternoon, and I'm at home. Where else? It's a rainy day. I'm in the dining-room. Mummy sits in her green baize armchair, feet stretched out as if they yearn for a footstool. Lunch is over. Chopped liver. Chicken, not quite brown enough. Butterbeans, hot, solid, swimming in pale sauce. Butter bean juice. Through the net curtains I see the bare branches of the plane tree in the back garden. A lively squirrel disobeys a rule they told me about in school - that squirrels hibernate through winter. This one crawls along a branch, leaps on another, swings perilously, hits a lower branch, hops to safety.

Lorna comes into the room looking normal that is until she sees me at which point she frowns darkly. The frown flowers into a sunny smile as Mummy turns and says to her:

"Hello darling."

"I thought we were having a Hebrew Lesson," says Lorna my big sister, aged thirteen.

Now we are at the dining room table. Lorna, Daddy and I peer at our books. Old books, I think, with sand coloured covers, and on the front this word: Aleh. This is Hebrew. Go up. Ascend. Go to the higher place. Lorna begins to read. Oniyah. A boat. There is a picture of a boat, which has a deck. "Oniyah. Al hasipun omed ish. Ish oleh l'Eretz Yisrael."

"What does that mean, girls?" Daddy asks us - beaming. It means the world to him, this sitting at the table, this Shabbat afternoon, giving us a Hebrew lesson. We say the words together and separately. Lorna starts, I start, then with that toss of black hair she interrupts and takes over, until I get back in the race somehow and we end together. A boat. On the deck stands a man. A man is going up to the land of Israel.

Friday Night. Eight O'clock.

I saw eternity the other night,
Like a great ring of pure and endless light.

I brought this Henry Vaughan poem home from school on Friday, which by sunset became "Friday Night" different from other nights. I tried to share it with Mum and Dad, with Lorna, who was now sixteen, but all they did was laugh.

"The point being," Mummy said, who was still Mummy to Lorna, Mum when I could manage it in the outside world, Mummy at home maybe. Vanessa

Price called her mother Mama, which I found quite stylish. "The point being . . ."

"What did you say the point was being?" Daddy asked, scratching his head, and my parents and my sister laughed together. So there was no discussion. Here was how it went, frequently. Not, I had discovered, when Lorna wanted to bring up serious questions of Jewish observance, or Mummy and Daddy wanted to talk about Israel. But when I attempted to import a Metaphysical Poet, the prose of Henry James, or the contemporary style of TS Eliot, there was hilarity around it. And as for my hoped for appointment to office? Secretary of English Club, under the chairmanship of Vanessa Price? The hilarity expressed, the peals of laughter - well, they blew tiles off the roof.

"Why is everyone laughing?"

"We're not," said Lorna.

Another Shabbat Afternoon. Four o'clock.

A different autumnal afternoon soon after. Eternity lay snug and forgotten inside my paperback collection, Metaphysical Poets. But this was the Shabbat on which my life changed, so I think of it as The Shabbat of the Metaphysical Poets. Drama, played out against a backcloth that was as metaphysical as any poem. Yet it wasn't. It was palpable, alive.

The backcloth was Shabbat still writ in Hebrew. There was I, both play and audience in a theatre where the mise-en-scene was my own home. White tablecloth, best crockery, last night's candles burned down in the silver candlesticks, leaving little piles of wax around the bases. For years to come, my memories will flutter back, moths to flames. This day (I was fourteen) was the last real Shabbat of my life. It contained the structure, colour, smells, all the themes. Later, when I will no longer observe the day in this way, it will replay itself in stored compartments of my brain. Little spools of memory in neat rows, with lids on.

"What are you girls doing tonight?" Daddy asked, with twinkling good humour. He had no idea that behind the cheerful facade of his daughters' holy demeanour, lay crocodile swamps of dirt. That was the question. What are you girls doing tonight? It was accompanied by the sound of a boy's name, which thudded in my head. Benjamin Brown. Benjamin Brown.

"It's complicated," Lorna sang sweetly, her eyes furrowing.

"You could phone Simone Cohen," Mummy suggested, but she must have known that this suggestion would be laughed out of court. Simone, the only other Jewish girl at our school. She was closer to me in age than to Lorna, but outside school she socialised with Lorna. It was like that with my friends. They were picked up, entertained, appropriated by her.

"Shabbat isn't out yet," said Lorna in her I'm-more-religious-than-you tone of voice.

Mummy and Daddy, bless them - as I continued to do long after I stopped believing in blessings but continued to like the phrase. Bless him. Bless her. Bless them. Mummy and Daddy did not have a clue. Benjamin Brown had done something the previous week which was vividly on my mind, Sabbath or no Sabbath. Aren't Sabbaths meant for witches, chirped witty Vanessa Price after French one day.

Benjamin Brown caught hold of me half way down Beckridge Road. He pulled me close, and kissed my lips. The mists and mellow fruits of autumn swirled around us, and I closed my mouth because the sensation of this teenage mouth on mine was tuggingly unpleasant. That is to say, I was tugged, hard, in two directions at once. Yes there was the tingle of pride that I was the one he chose to kiss. I didn't push him away. The notion, that of standing on a dark pavement, my sister Lorna walking off in the dark, the notion was an excellent one, the concept perfect. But the kiss itself? I thought he might have sand on his lips. Ash berries cascaded over the stone garden wall behind us, bright red under the street lighting.

That was last Sunday. Monday we met on the stairs, me and Lorna. I apologised because Benjamin Brown had kissed me. Actually apologised. Then Lorna revealed she was devastated because she really did like him herself. At which I instantly felt mortified and guilty, because all these years, there had been this absolute droit de grande soeur, hadn"t there. "Lorna is our firstborn!" Lorna first, me second. That's how it felt to me.

Tuesday on the way to school I explained that I did indeed like Benjamin myself, I did but frankly felt shy – and not sure what should happen next.

"I do definitely know that he likes you," Lorna said, wielding authority gently, thoughtfully, as if she had heard this from the horse's mouth, from the boy himself, who had slate grey eyes and a stare like a cowboy's.

"Tell you what," she offered on Thursday, the week whizzing by, "why don't I talk to him? I get on fine with him. We talk about things. He told me he does like you, he really does. But he's worried about the fact that you are . . . this is what he said . . . inexperienced."

"Inexperienced!" The most exciting word I had ever heard. It could only mean one thing! Experience was on the agenda. It had to be. From inexperience, would come experience! It would have to!

Lorna had saved my life once, grabbing me as a car swept by on Kings Road. So now I did the defeated animal thing. I put my head back. I exposed my bare neck to the wolf's teeth. I allowed myself to feel protected by, nurtured by my big sister. This Saturday night I believed she would meet with Benjamin Brown. They would discuss how he and I might become closer and kiss again.

Shabbat/Saturday Afternoon. Three o'clock. I am in the Central library because Vanessa Price, chair of English Club gave me, secretary at last, almost seventeen, in the sixth form, the task of choosing a play for our next meeting. My brain buzzes with the challenge. I'm looking at Androcles and the Lion by

George Bernard Shaw. On the table I've put Julia Carey's favourite writer. Charles Morgan.

I move round libraries, bookshops, a bit like a ghost in a film. Indistinctly, there but not there. That's me with English literature. I gravitate towards poetry and plays but something pulls me away, steers me to the more sensible topics that are discussed at home. Languages. She could teach languages. When we're all living in Israel, she can teach English. Music. If she practised more she could become a piano teacher. I look round uneasily, my stomach cramping, sigh inwardly. There is a deep knowledge in me about all this. It hasn't found its words yet in any language.

I'll write my diary tonight, after I've walked home, after Shabbat. Meanwhile I'm hunched over Life in Seventeenth Century France, marveling at the excesses of Louis Quatorze, the Sun King. For his evening meal alone, the Sun King consumed four plates of soup, a whole pheasant, a partridge, slices of ham, mutton with garlic, a plate of pastry, followed by fruit, washed down with champagne. Imagine. On the subject of excesses I too am fat now. I began to eat a lot just after the thing happened. Is that why thinking of Louis Quatorze my mouth begins to water? I imagine the appetite he must have had. Also, I feel curious about the ham.

Vanessa is here in the library. She's at her deep mahogany desk, scribbling away in exotic handwriting, head dipped in concentration. She gets up, to stretch and say hello, standing tall, rippling brown curls festooning her poetic face. Vanessa was born to be both Prefect and Head Girl. She is sylphlike and athletic, and plays royalty in every school play – kings and queens. She is related to a member of the current cabinet whose identity she is not free to divulge. Seeking ways to connect, I reminded her at the last English Club meeting that Virginia Woolf's husband was Jewish. Leonard.

"I know," she mused, "Miss Meadows wondered whether Virginia drowned herself partly because of all that, you know. The marriage . . ." What did that mean? I did not ask. Vanessa Lara Price was and always will be everything I am not.

I composed a poem to Miss Meadows, Head of English, about God wanting me to learn to write in a different language. There was a family plan, I wrote, drawn up before my birth. A hundred years ago in Lithuania. Revived every Shabbat afternoon at home, at the home end of the school week. Aleh! Go up to the Land of Israel.

Saturday Afternoon. Three o'clock.

I'm at my desk, in my student digs. It is December. I'm at a red brick university in a hilly northern city. The air smells of frosted smoke, or smoked frost. Dead leaves freeze on the steep pavements and crunch underfoot. I'm a student of Philosophy because I did not dare to walk through the door named "English." I have Descartes open in front of me. To my right, Kant's Critique of Pure Reason unopened.

I'm half way through an essay. I started it yesterday afternoon, Friday, in the university library. A narrowing alcove had drawn me to a poorly lit corner, to a desk that was almost hidden. Above me I caught sight of a blue volume, "Mystics Through History."

I started writing at three fifty-five, knowing that Shabbat would begin in five minutes. It was my intention to keep writing, but at four o'clock the shadows of past lives and laws fell across the opening lines of my essay, Time In Philosophy. When it felt their weight my hand stopped writing. Images drifted across the A4 page, and its thin blue lines began to wriggle like water, inviting me to keep writing, but lives and laws flowed across them, detritus on the surface of the river. History, I suppose. History, and faces. Images floated by.

Here was Daddy, about to chant Havdalah, the prayer for that dividing moment between the end of Shabbat and the rest of the week, between day and night, between Jews and other nations. Here were Lorna and myself tripping out into the garden to check the sky for the required three stars, because he could not begin to chant the space between us and the wide world until we spied three stars in the firmament.

There was Lorna, composed and thoughtful. Until the three stars, the chanting, she looked so comfortable, so embedded in our inherited day of rest. Then, Daddy sang the Hebrew words, holding up a silver cup of milk. He passed round the tub of sweet-smelling herbs, which we sniffed, each of us, in honour of the sweet week ahead. Lorna was at peace whether she deserved to be or not. And there was Mummy, sitting at the kitchen table, after Havdalah. She will be smiling at us forever, carefully cleaning cold wax from the candlesticks.

Open the door to one memory, another slips through. This one is of Lorna, on the verge of leaving home but still there, longing for her sweet week to begin after Shabbat, because Benjie (Benjie!) said he would call and they might go out. Your so-called boyfriend is unreliable! Mummy and Daddy are so sympathetic I can't bear it.

Wait till you're living in Jerusalem, girls, they comfort both of us. Lorna for Benjamin Brown's heartlessness, me for what Mummy calls That Look. I cannot bear that look, she says, and looks away herself. Wait till you're living in Jerusalem, they say again hopefully. Jerusalem will comfort us all. My parents.

Yesterday the spirit of Shabbat followed me into the University Library. I put down the pen because I could not make it move on the paper. I walked back to my digs, jumbled memories of the adolescence I had left behind pounding in my head. A bus went by, and I was drawn to jump on it, crash through the barrier of Sabbath observance but my feet wouldn't lift.

But then last night I dreamed about climbing a hill, and birds singing, and this morning I woke up thinking that yesterday in the library I had suc-cumbed to weakness, nothing worse. Then all of a sudden the break happened. I jumped out of bed, grabbed a piece of paper and wrote: "Hello, me." That's how easy it was in the end.

And now, I'm sitting here writing on Shabbat! The pen is moving. These actual words are being committed to paper.

"Yesterday," I confide in my flatmate Meg, who is plucking her eyebrows, "I somehow had to put my pen down when I knew Shabbat was starting."

"Me, I'm proud to be Jewish," says Meg, "but I don't do all that stuff."

"What about Israel?" I ask. Still can't help sounding superior on the topic.

"I went once. Didn't like it. Far too hot, for a start."

"Lorna is there now," I note. Because she is. Two thousand miles away, in a small flat in Jerusalem, with her happy headscarf, devout husband, and pregnant belly. Believe it or not, I wish her happiness.

Fifty Years Later. Tuesday Morning.

The day I stood in our pingpong cellar, waiting for Lorna and Benjamin Brown to come in from the back garden, where - hard to believe, I know, but I did - they were talking one more time (ha ha) about how he would approach me so our teenage love (it would become love) would finally blossom. The day my eyes saw them come inside, Lorna red-faced, grinning, Benjamin steely-eyed as ever. The day she pulled away from his embrace, tugged her white cardigan round her shoulders, then came over to me and whispered in my ear, "Don't worry. It'll be your turn next time."

How I struggled not to feel betrayed and heart-broken for four whole years. Week in, week out, Friday night to Shabbat to Sunday rambles and the odd sweaty outing to a smoky jazz club. We few, we happy few, eh? So very few of us. Half a dozen? A dozen? No air to breathe.

There was, of course, the poetic but shabby Franklin, brown-eyed, scruffy beard, who went around with Sylvia Plath under his arm. He brought the dark dimension – his father had been in Buchenwald. One Christmas, Simone Cohen hosted a party. We all went, all eleven of us. To the pounding of I Wanna Hold Your Hand, Franklin and I kissed hotly, and that was actually fine. But after the event, if you can call it that, I didn't know what to do with myself, and hunched on the grey sofa, waiting to see what would happen. He'd found a doorway to stand in from where he began to declaim,

I saw eternity the other night,
Like a great ring of pure and endless light

So I arose, and floated towards him, warmed from the kissing upstairs, offering my actual soul, overjoyed to have found at last a kindred spirit. But looking down his nose at me, he declaimed, "Someone get that silly cow out of here, so I can finish this poem of sublime beauty!" And everyone laughed. Everyone.

As for Benjamin Brown, he flitted in and out of our very small group, driving Lorna crazy. I didn't mind that. Once he said to me, seven of us on a ramble in a wood full of bluebells, "If you lost weight I'd be after you again myself!" I blushed heavily and trudged on.

That day. The Day, a second year student, I broke free, to inhabit a new universe, become a new person. Shabbat would now be Saturday for ever. I was still plump but I stopped getting fatter. And in adult life, you will believe this or not, I became as normal and happy as anyone. Good genes, good parents, and a sister I do really love. Only I still tend not to tolerate people who believe too much – in anything.

The Dressmaker

"Do come in," says Madame Colette Safran, beckoning. A narrow corridor with a rich dark carpet leads to her workroom. The walls are lined with photographs in diamond studded frames. Women look radiant in fashionable settings. Celebrities, ball gowns, sequins, men in bow ties. This could be a dream, except it isn't.

"So. Tell me how I can help you."

"I have this dress. I bought it for a friend's wedding. Then I found the front was too low. For me, that is – personally. Embarrassingly low."

"Really?" She raises an eyebrow. "Let us regard the offending garment!"

Her accent is French, I think. Or Belgian. She eases the dress out of its cover, rests it over the back of a crimson chaise-longue. It lies there, limp, innocuous. Her posture is erect, soothing. Something in her dark, watchful eyes, gently regal smile. Out begins to pour a veritable Curriculum Vitae.

Myself. My mother – my late mother. My husband. Our sons. Our daughter. I relate how Julia strayed for a while. Goth, anarchist, cannabis, born-again, she is now a college librarian with an interest in refugees.

"And tell me," purrs this dressmaker I selected from Yellow Pages Online, "more about the dress. "You say that your dear mother instructed you to find a dressmaker?"

Have I already told her that? I have been babbling.

She did. Almost the last thing she told me - hours before she died. She died months ago. I'm supposed to have passed the first stages of mourning, as they refer to it in books. I'm supposed to be remembering the good things. Tears threaten.

This is the moment when I turn my head, and spy six pale, anxious looking women gathered around me. I frown at the first one who frowns back. Look again and see the same woman to my right. Same to the left. And one over there in the corner. I notice the shabby tunic-top. Mine. Colette Safran's work room is not simply hung with a mirror or two, as you would expect. Three walls are made of two mirrors each, nothing but mirrors. In the last mirror this woman, late sixties, coarse hair that needs a trim turns towards me. Accusingly.

"Et alors . . ." Colette gathers our green dress softly on her outstretched arms. I fix my gaze on her so I won't have to stare at these six illuminated versions of me. They stand in tight pantie-girdles, long bras cutting into their shoulders, stomachs bulging between edges of bras and girdles. And their legs. Not that fat, actually but far too white. Veinous estuaries above the knees gleam blue and purple. Our Almost Black Support Socks look dense, obsidian, vulgar.

"Voilà!" Colette seems relaxed, unlike the six women whose faces now freeze in one tight, puzzled, determined expression. Like my mother at the moment of death. She sat up straight then, her mouth set stiff, not going gentle into any dark night thank you, eyes glaring, wide.

Mirrors surround me. The women in the mirrors share one expression. A brightly illuminated one. I'm slipping into a cage of cold light. Self-reflection. At my age!

The mirror on the left flickers, to get my attention. I turn round, my face close to Colette's. She is manicured, poised, made up. Me, I never wear make-up. I look my age; people stand up for me on the tube. Colette positions herself behind me. I feel the pressure of her hands on my shoulders, as she pulls the dress half an inch higher. "I will," she explains, "simply hitch it up on the shoulders, and then the low V will no longer be low!" When I wear it again no-one will get that view, the sweaty creek between my two big breasts.

"So." I take off the green floral dress, fling it on the chaise-longue, put trousers and shirt on quickly, whip brush out of shabby handbag and run it through my hair.

"We need to arrange a time for a fitting. When is convenient?"

I am standing, my back to the mirrors, my eyes on the front door, but I sense movement in them nevertheless. My six doppelgangers frown in their reverse universe, their mouths open and close. I feel cold. I don't want this. But I don't intend to panic, just because I am in a roomful of mirrors. I take out my diary and we plan the next fitting.

"That will be delightful," she says.

We're saying goodbye. I wish Colette would close the workroom door but she doesn't so I am still at the mercy of the mirrors. The women seem wary, watchful. As I withdraw and they distance them-selves I think they are whispering. To my relief they retreat, turning back into their mirror world, but next thing someone comes skipping past them towards me. A small figure. Yes, a small figure runs, leaping towards me.

That is me! I'm five. My hair is dazzling auburn. I'm in the park. My body, my one and only own little body is perfect. It can do anything. I can jump, skip and hop. My mother is peeling a banana for me, my first one!

I walk shakily out past the thyme and mint, real scents mingling with those coming back to life in Colette Safran's work room. As the front door closes, I hear her phone ringing - the old-fashioned filigree silver version. I may be shaking but I'll have to return.

Tuesday, she welcomes me like a friend. She slips the dress on me, casually, and the mirrors light up. I stand stiffly, view myself in all the mirrors at once. Six identical images. Or not. Not exactly. Out of one corner, out of the grey glassy background, some movement, it's here, in the second mirror. A figure is slowly coming into view. Is this a spirit, a dream? No, not at all. It is me again, growing up now. What am I doing? I'm hurtling towards myself. Here I come. From fifteen to sixty-nine, teenage me races towards the present.

Or not. Not that either. Not out of the mirror. Teenage me is running just the way I did then. I run in and out of my childhood home. I am sprinting, panting, as I did then. From front door, to kitchen, to biscuit tin, then back to front door. Yes, running, panting. Oh no, God no. Before my eyes – this is the day I couldn't stop eating ginger biscuits.

Madame's hands smooth the dress, to subdue a wrinkle, no a wave, no the tidal wave of chiffon which has appeared since my last visit here. There might be a fault, she says frowning. The alteration isn't working yet.

Can't she smell the ginger-biscuits? They are in the cubbyhole in the kitchen dresser of my childhood. I'm at the front door, it's half past one, time to catch the bus back to school. Summer time. My emerald uniform skirt tightens week by week. This might be what teenage pregnancy feels like but I'm not pregnant. Only pregnant with frustrations, hatred of my sister, resentment of my mother who tells me to eat when I'm not hungry and to stop eating when I am. All the while I'm getting fatter.

The house stands between bus stops. Till now it was a game. You hear the bus stopping at Woodhouse Road, which means you have two minutes in which to run, in advance of it, to the St Katherine's stop and get there, panting, ahead. An obsession I share with my sister, who today is not here. She's at school skipping lunch losing weight. The family pattern. We go like this: fat thin fat thin, mother daughter sister cousin. See us at weddings and Christmases.

I nip back inside to get a third ginger biscuit, then stand at the front door, sun on face, and crunch. My great monster of a greedy soul tumbles in the sky, swooping down to capture me in a tornado of need so strong that it lifts me a foot in the air. Keep eating biscuits until the bus comes.

I do. I do. And incredibly that same scene replays itself whole, all these years later, in Colette Safran's mirrors. There I go. Crunch munch watch for bus. Run inside, flip cubbyhole, get biscuit, reach porch, gobble, glance at road, then run back for another one. Like a panting puppy, I play the game over, over and over.

"Et voila! I see how to solve our problem." With Colette's voice the taste of ginger leaves my lips. "You will need to come back for another fitting. You will look wonderful."

"Thank you for your hard work," I smile falsely. She clasps my hands warmly but I pull away. I could dislike this innocent dressmaker I hardly know.

§

Julia called earlier. For some reason - never happened before - she asked me about the dress, the dressmaker, and we got on to wedding dresses. She asked me what mine had been like. Plain, I said, and on we chatted. I mentioned that my mother had motioned to me not to speed towards the bridal canopy. "Don't run," she'd whispered, a twinkle in her eye, "Not seemly!"

It's Wednesday afternoon, two minutes to three. I've had time since the last fitting to reflect carefully on what is happening. I have a theory, so I skip past the thyme and mint. I know that today there will be a different scene in the mirror. A sweet one, and it will make me happy. Because my body did not remain unlovable, did it? Oh no definitely no. How could I have forgotten! Size eighteen or not, I found love. I found love, and it found love too.

So today I will seek out that body in the mirror, and ignore the irritation of Colette's fingers, tugging gently at flaps of cloth that have still not disappeared. I won't mind if the dress is not yet satisfactory. In fact I hope it isn't.

Because today I'm here willingly. Today I peer eagerly, my eyes avoiding hers. My past plays brightly in her mirrors, and it is my good fortune to have been alerted to this. Yes, there I am. I'm ~~there~~ in a white wedding dress, my husband beside me looking nervous. There is my mother, radiant in her fifties. Years younger than I am now! She puts out a hand. "Don't run, darling! It isn't seemly."

"We will need yet another fitting," Colette's voice comes from very far-away.

I'm immersed, now, in this game, I'm learning. The mirrors want to play with my past? Let them. I'll play too. And I'll choose my own moments.

Such as this one now, for example. Yes, this one. Here I am, moving purposefully through the glass walls of dressmaker time towards one night I want to remember. Through the shadows I see that night. My moment of walking across a shabby landing. It is that landing. The only reality now is on this landing. That night. What happens that night? We've been together two or three years. We are building what people call a marriage, although I don't see it, myself, this thing with that name. I see us.

We have a small furnished house on the outskirts of the city. The floors are made of lino which has an uneven relationship with the walls. Lino. Never quite fitting snug. Dark stains where moisture gets in. Damp from the windows, spilt coffee, spilt wine. I'm on the landing, my feet cold on the threadbare carpet. Floral patterns, between rhododendrons and roses. Patches of bare carpeting create dull-brown puddles.

I'm walking across this landing, musing. Only men believe thinking and bodies belong in different spheres. What happened, in there? That room? I turn round, and see the end of the bed, the Portuguese bedspread I bought for five pounds. Malcolm's feet splayed in the half-light. In the middle of three sensational orgasms, best ever, I'd been asking questions. Who are we. Who is he. Who am I. Who was I. Who will I become.

Will I ever feel this again, this particular sensation of damp, richly scented Being Alive in the middle of a night? What are the smells? Walking on a forest floor perhaps. Rich dark mossy perfumes.

I stand at the cracked sink and turn on the tap. I see the flannel and soap. Imperial Leather. The flannel is brand new, the water hot, and I wash myself slowly, luxuriously. Two hooks wobble on faded tiles with blackened grouting. Whoever hammered them in, whoever those people were, they lived in a very grubby house. Me, I live in a palace.

By now I am half asleep, ready to go back to bed, and cover my husband's sleeping body. That's what he does - falls asleep after sex, wakes up an hour later saying it's cold. An answer inscribes itself across my inner eye, even though I'm so drowsy I no longer know what the question was. But the answer is a shout out, a revelation, a resolution. "We are at peace, my body and I. There is peace between us."

"I'm happy with it, as it is," I tell Colette today, who keeps passing her thin fingers over the material, instructing it to behave.

"You may be happy my dear but me, I am a perfectionist."

As I drive to the next fitting, I am in labour. By the time Madame Safran is inspecting her handiwork, checking whether she has it right this time, I am ready to give birth, one more time, to Julia! The miracle of the mirrors I'll call it. I stare. My selves stare back. Then the pictures come.

Midwives, nurses, everyone dancing, and I'm singing. The slow movement of Beethoven's Choral Symphony. The rise and fall of the melody matches my contractions.

People in white wipe faces and hand me Julia. My girl after two boys. Slippery but snug, carried by my body and ushered by it out into the world, Malcolm beside us looking pale. The smells of fresh sweet blood, disinfectant, sweat, dissipate as Colette's voice closes a curtain over the mirrors. She's sweet, actually. I'm having a great time. Next week, another fitting.

§

I've absolutely got it. I understand what is happening. I've been entertaining myself in Colette's massive mirrors as a protection against anxiety. I would otherwise be far too fraught forced to gaze upon my half-naked self. Six magnifications of my body in merciless light. This week I come with a jewel of a scenario in mind. I thought of it in the shower last night.

I am forty-three. My mother is sixty-nine, the age I am now. Julia is eleven. We are having a day out in Hampton Court, and my mother has provided the picnic. Her face is flushed in the sun, her arms harsh red in places, because when it's hot - we don't know if it's insects or not - she scratches obsessively. White skin, capillaries staining it at the slightest irritation.

"I've brought the same for each of us!" She puts three melamine plates on the grass. Two sandwiches, crisps, three pickled cucumbers, two tomatoes, three rounded fish balls on each plate.

"No fish balls thank you," says Julia critically.

"But we're all having the same! Don't you see? Why not have three like the rest of us!" My mother thinks Julia is too thin and it's my fault. We're swinging in a food chain of fish balls on a sunny day in a park and it goes on. At the end, Julia's plate still holds a mountain of uncrunched crisps. My mother looks troubled.

"Your crisps, Julia. Do finish them. Look - our plates are empty!"

Colette seems to think she has solved the problem. One more fitting and the dress will be perfect. All she needs to do is unpick it again. She gathered too much material on this side, here. Literally a centimetre or two.

"It would help," she says, "if you could stand up straight. And do me one favour. Don't keep tugging at your bra strap." But I can't do what she asks. And why should I? I'm too uncomfortable.

"Please," she repeats. "Your strap."

But like that day years ago when my will gave way to the ginger biscuits, it now gives way again. My reflections and I are unable to refrain from pulling at our bra straps, which slide inexorably over our shoulder bones - which are not like other people's. They are crushed. Our hands tug, stretching the dress a little. She is trying to help us, I see that she cares, but we eye Colette defiantly.

"This is getting out of hand." she observes coolly. "For some reason, you will not relax. Please. Do me the favour of becoming calm. Ma pauvre, you are tired of these fittings."

I assure her benignly that I'm having a great time.

My six reflections catch me in the lie, and we all smile with irony.

Their faces. All six of them, with that same self-knowing smug smile. Are they with me, these reflections, or against me? This time I drive away with a sense of having been caught out. Back home I can't stop thinking about them. Their persistence, their ability to focus. Presumably I deserve their displeasure.

§

Warily, I have come for the last-but-one fitting. Colette busies herself with a new problem, her back to me, leaving me alone, half dressed, surrounded by my several selves. This time I look at them with real coolness, and they look back at me coldly. It's as if they want something. They glare, all of them, with the same searching glint. Six pairs of eyes.

I put up a hand, in a gesture, and they all raise their hands at me. But then, suddenly, we split, we separate, yolks from whites, or whites from yolks, and they're free, or I am, or actually I'm not, because now they're beckoning, they're calling me, all of them, and in this moment of weakness I become theirs.

They reach out, pull me, out of the crimson room, and into the other place, their cold reflected world. I am drawn by the shameful betrayal of my very own reflections, to the room, the bed on which my mother lay an hour before she died.

§

I'm here early. I'm beside our mother on the day of her death. Again. From nine in the morning, I sit by her, in the small hospice ward that has opened its arms to us. My sister is due at one. My mother and I have until then. She is hooked up to oxygen, and some morphine. She says quietly, "I was going to ask you to put the post in a pile, and I'd sort it out when I get home. But then I thought: oh no, I won't be going home."

Rattling behind me comes from a trolley wheeled in by a bearded elder in a Stetson Hat. I read "Professor Edwards" on his name tag.

"Morning tea, ma'am?" this volunteer asks.

"Do you have cold milk?"

"Ask the nurses," he says. "What would you like for lunch?"

"What is there?

"Soup. Fish. Potatoes. Green beans."

"Is the soup hot?" my mother asks assertively. He inclines his head.

"It will be so."

"What were you a professor of?" my voice asks as if it means something, which surprisingly turns out to be the case.

"Geology," he replies, scratching his beard. I think of mountain ranges, valleys and rock-faces and that the universe is billions of years old.

"Find a nurse, darling. I'd like a glass of milk." Nurses are plentiful here, and I find one immediately. The milk is full fat and cold, and my mother drinks it with appreciation.

"Was that all right?"

"Another, please." I witness my mother drinking two glasses of milk at eleven o'clock, then hot soup at twelve - I steady the spoon. With my help she samples more than half of fried fish mashed potatoes and green beans. And I read her thoughts: I am calm because of the morphine, relaxed by the oxygen, but here's a discovery. My appetite is not bad, under the circumstances. I may be in a hospice, but I surely have a few good days left.

No. Within an hour she will be dead, handled roughly by the ultrasound technician who will kill her by making her lie flat - so the fluid in her lungs will burst like a dam and flood her heart.

That hasn't happened yet. At this moment, I'm experiencing an existentially illuminating revelation. I am counting the thousand connections between the threads of life, motherhood, food and bodies.

We set off for the ultra-sound department. She is jolted from side to side of the corridor as the geologist wheels the iron bed-on-wheels, followed by me and now my sister who has to my immense relief come early.

The first time our mother dies my sister stays heroically beside her but can't stop shaking. Myself,

I run away, too terrified. What kind of a mother is this, who has not taught us to accept her ending?

"Help us!" I shriek down the empty corridor.

I turn back into the moment, my heart thumping, and here is where the scene takes root, establishes itself, embeds itself. From now, it will simply keep happening. My mother dying her indelible death. Her eyes roll back, right into her head. Her poor poor head.

And me? I wish I had been able to show some real solidarity, in the face of shock, instead of all that shrieking, leaping, escaping, shaking! But that's the way it truly was. That scene happened. So from now and for always it will roll like a box-office hit the minute it finds an opportunity.

The truth. Look at myself in any mirror, with honesty, and it will be there. So I nod towards my reflections, and they nod back. It's a draw, I suppose. Or stalemate or checkmate between me and them. Is that me, or them, smiling in that grim and finally knowing way?

§

"Just for my satisfaction, try this on one more time." Colette's voice is crisp, assertive, but I refuse. So she sets about folding the dress, then swaddles it in tissue paper, finally placing it in a gold-fringed paper carrier-bag. Instead of handing me the bag, she sits down, folds her arms, and nods, as if expecting me to sit down too, and say something to her. Perhaps she wants me to explain my obsessive staring at her glass walls.

But I say my goodbyes standing, then turn to leave. I open the front door, and see bees circling the herbs. She follows me to the path outside. I hold out my hand, take hers. I thank her for her devoted work, then out I go. I open the car, and toss the gold-fringed bag onto the back seat.

Words

Writers need to swim in a language, like wicked sharks in the deep. Take us out of the ocean of words and we start to die.

— *Rosie*, by Rose Tremain

The pilot asked us not to use phones until we were out of the aircraft, but no one took any notice. Ringtones from familiar to esoteric ring out and echo down the aisle.

"Hello Mummy! I've landed." I look round uneasily. Thirty-five years ago my parents and sisters left England, to make Israel their home. At that time, it was natural for us all to call Mummy Mummy. A middle-class British family thing. But now I am almost sixty. My children call me Mum at home, Ma as a joke, Mother in public. But over the years I have found it hard to stop calling my mother Mummy. I've worked out as follows. My sisters, Rina and Tamar, held on to Mummy because in Hebrew mothers begin as Ima and remain Ima forever. No need for a change of name.

I am squashed in the aisle, hemmed in by teenage boys on one side, a woman with a baby on the other, a loud-voiced businessman in front of us.

"Muki!" he barks to his purple phone, "Tafsik! Maspik!" Stop it. Enough.

§

The taxi-ride is like a colour film even though it is night-time. Beside me two Russian women appear to be in love. I envy their language, it sounds so rich.

"Sh-zj stdrazniet nayo szjink masskvitchka!" One of them peels a clementina, which is what I called these fruits when I lived here. Now I call them clementines, or more often tangerines.

In a passion of soft fingers, one slips orange segments through her lover's wet lips. I hear a shy giggle. I imagine pips quivering on her tongue. We're driving through dark hills to Jerusalem.

In the seat behind me there is Madame Yvette, who hands me a business card. She is a tourist guide from Alexandria on her way to Bethlehem. Her ruby cross catches moonlight through the taxi window. Her hair is covered with sequined netting.

"I will take the Holy Mass," she tells me, "à la mémoire de mon père."

The woman beside the driver is called Avital. They talk in Hebrew about depression in America and opioids. His favourite singer is Amy Winehouse. I interrupt to tell them I live only four miles away from where she lived – and died. In London. When he bends to find the CD, the taxi swerves alarmingly. Back to Black starts to play, and Avital rests her head on his shoulder. I imagine she'll take him to her flat.

He hoots at a Palestinian woman carrying lemons and ropes. The Russians jettison peel like confetti. Mist covers my entry into the city and my ears ache. By a garage, a guide dog watches. I see men in black hats, shoppers, and some young soldiers.

§

Rina is waiting as the taxi pulls up, and makes squeaks of joy.

"Give me a hug! Let me take your case!" I visit Jerusalem frequently, so I have keys. The outer door. The lift key. Then the door key. But tonight we don't need the door key. Mummy flings open the door, and I am inside, looking round at the familiar furniture, the books, the pictures on the wall. Something happens to my eyes when I come here. They see differently. She is in her dressing-gown.

"It's all right. I am ready for bed, that's all. I wanted to stay up for you, but I thought I'd make it easier for myself. Rina, are you making a cup of tea? Come and see Daddy – he's almost asleep."

They are old; he is ninety-four, she eighty-six. Time has gone by and only Rina talks as if nothing is wrong or could ever be. Rina lives in the best of all possible worlds, and Jerusalem is the best of all cities.

"Miriam's here," Mummy says to Daddy, who opens his eyes, beams, murmurs, "Hello darling. Long journey. I'll be out of here soon."

"What does he mean?" Rina whispers.

"He's half asleep," Mummy says quietly, "probably dreaming he's out shopping or something."

§

"I've brought you a present," I tell my mother, and she laughs.

"No need for presents!"

"It wasn't heavy. I've brought three, so you'll have choices. Or maybe give one to Tamar, one to Rina, and keep one."

"Ah! Dye!" she exclaims happily, and takes out my gift. Or gifts. Three in one if she likes, or just three. "Black. Dark Navy. Smoke Grey," Rina reads the small packets.

"You are the only one of my daughters who dyes things," Mummy remarks, "and sometimes I envy you for it! Now I have to decide whether it's my white skirt or my pink nightie."

We chat about dyeing things. I recall a moment in my therapy – I had therapy for three years once - and my therapist saying smilingly that we play tricks on ourselves with words. Words are messages, she insisted, but we don't always decipher them. I didn't take her that seriously, but I do take seriously that as soon as I land here, in Jerusalem, my mind plays tricks on me. My parents' home here is not the home I grew up in, which was in Southern England. I was used to being one piece in a jigsaw. Then suddenly I became a different piece. The crockery signifies home, from salad servers to mugs to breadboard to cereal bowls, and the bowls will last forever – they're pyrex. But it isn't the crockery. It's me.

Next day I go to the makolet to get milk and rolls. Outside, the boundaries of the person who is me flicker, flounder like the ground I am on. My eyes close, and pinpoints of light spread, then, and I'm half floating. I feel like an angel in an old film. I say to myself, it's my ears - first the flight, then Jerusalem being so high up. But I know it isn't.

§

Daddy is very ill, and there is a chamsin. Not just a warm dry wind. My mother has put on the air-conditioner, the on-off mode. Just when you get used to the background hum, it ceases, and silence fills the air. Twenty minutes later, you are comfortable in the silence, and there is a click like a knock at a door and the hum comes back.

Rina comes in each morning to chat about her day. Her Jerusalem day. Each day there is some comment, she can't help it, Jerusalem is in her blood, as it was once supposed to be in mine, except with me it leaked out, faded - that sense of comfort and ownership. Rina was born in England but the day she set foot in Jerusalem she belonged here. I didn't leave England until I was twenty-two – armed with a Philosophy degree.

Rina kisses Daddy on the forehead. His electric mattress moves gently through the day so he won't get sore. I imagine he might feel like a boat at sea, but he isn't telling us.

"Bye darling, have a good day," he says. He is lucid this morning. I am proud of them. Proud of Mummy, the way she looks after Daddy, of Daddy for the way he looked after us.

At midday Tamar arrives laden with goodies. Sultana cake, fishballs, a roast chicken cradled in carrots and peppers.

"How is your beautiful lemon tree?" Mummy admires the abundance of foods.

"We can't use it this year," Tamar doesn't look reproachful, because we are not a family of reproach, but the reminder is there. It is the Shemitah year.

"Now that is something I never think about at home," I say unapologetically. "As you know." Of course they know. But I tend to say these things. Coded provocation, I suppose, in a Jewish, family-based kind of way. In England there is no such thing as Shemitah. Shemitah is the law about letting the earth lie fallow once every seven years. A biblical instruction given to us more than two thousand years before climate change.

"It is one of those Mitzvot," Tamar reminds me sunnily, "that we are instructed to observe properly now that we are all here." That slip of the tongue. We may be all here, at this moment in time. We're not all here in the deeper sense.

§

My father is weakening. This evening he is propped up, super-nourished. Mummy has brought tins of liquid food full of vitamins. He sucks from one through a bent straw. We watch him through this repast, but his glazed eyes keep glancing towards the window. I imagine he is imagining dying.

"Drink more, darling," Mummy urges him, now holding a cup of water to his lips but he turns his face away. "You'll be dehydrated if you don't drink," she murmurs, but then she puts the cup down. His weariness is unbearable.

Shortly after eight, he is asleep. Rina stays, Tamar is here overnight anyway, and we all sit down to watch the news. But half way through the news he wakes up, and begins calling. Mummy, Tamar, Miriam, Rina. So we switch off coverage of the old adversaries, Israelis and Palestinians, and what they've been up to today. Killings? None, unusually. The occupation, as always. An encounter. An imprisonment. A threat. Several threats. What does the news mean to him now? God of Jerusalem if you are here bring peace.

We go to him in the night. I go, Mummy goes, the nurse who comes at ten goes; Tamar stays over. At midnight there are crashes of thunder, flashings of lightning and the skies open. The wind has dried out the sky which cracks open like the desiccated ground. I sense strange combinations of liquids - mucus, urine, sweat, tears, blood, rain and more rain.

I sit with him for a while around three o'clock. Patterns of capillaries on his thin arm make miniature maps in the half-light. I touch his shoulder gently, and whisper, "Goodnight Daddy," then creep from the room. But in a flash he's awake, calling out to me with strangely renewed strength.

"Miriam. Go and wake Mummy up," he orders. "Get her to drink something or she'll be dehydrated."

"Mummy is asleep," I whisper shakily, "She's fine."

"No. Go to your mother, wake her, do as I say!" he orders.

"OK."

"Don't just say OK like that. Get her to drink or she will die."

"I think she needs to sleep. We all need to sleep." And he lies back for a moment, then starts again.

"To be honest, I am astonished! More astonished than I have ever been, at you! All I can say is – may heaven help you! You need the help of heaven."

Mummy has now woken with the shouting, and comes to him so I leave. Whispering, they urge each other to drink. Somehow I fall asleep. At dawn I'm up first, and first back in his room. He smiles and says hello darling.

But he's in a cell. I see it. A cell of thin skin and stiff bone. My curiosity is sharp, it's like a knife that cuts, but I seem to be indulging in self-harm with it. Otherwise why allow these thoughts? Is he dreaming, as he lies there, eyes closed, that reserved expression on his face, of all the cells he spent a life discovering? Microscopic, life-giving, minuscule? Does he remember his first golden career, his good strong days as A Renowned British Scientist? The journals, the conferences, the commitment to exploration of life's molecules and circulations? On and off trains to London he would go.

My mind slices through memories now the way Daddy used to slice through slides of blood cells, fat cells, nerve cells. Frozen sections, he explained to me. We call these frozen sections. We freeze them in order to keep things exactly as they are.

I remember the final celebratory trip we made to the lab, all three of us. There was an international congress, hosted by Daddy who was retiring and saying goodbye to England, and we were invited to attend the party. "I am proud to introduce you to my wife, and to my daughters. Tamar, Miriam and Rina."

I was filled with curiosity about the alchemies of modern science. I sensed the significance of Daddy's work, and felt admiration. And here was that American grandee we had been told about. "My American friend Harold . . ." He wore a name tag. Professor H S Mansfield.

"Professor Mansfield," Daddy stood beside me proudly, "is an important man. He sits on a committee that chooses whom to nominate for Nobel Prizes."

"And your father is a hero of haematology," Professor Mansfield retorted. "England will be sorry to lose him, but England's loss will be Israel's gain!"

Everything that night was falling into place. Tamar was already in Israel, on her kibbutz. Just home on a visit, she told everyone. Rina was excited, about to leave school. I will not be choosing an

English university, she told everyone. I am choosing Jerusalem.

And me? I was the floater. The fuzzy smudge that floated across their fields of vision, dimming their view of Daddy's post-retirement career in a top Israeli research institute – and their ideal of a family staying together, moving together. Going Home, they said. All of us.

I count homecomings. I think of opening the front door early evening, as he arrived home from the capital. He smiled at me warmly. Is Mummy in? Through the hall to the kitchen, he marched energetically. Through the door, across the red lino floor. He kissed her forehead, then turned back to sit down at the head of the kitchen table. His place in his house. The coffee grinder on the wall just above his head.

"I've brought the Evening Standard," he said casually, putting the newspaper down for my mother to pick up. The world out there was always England, London, conferences, newspapers, trains, meetings - then homecomings.

But here in the house, in a kind of magical manifestation, hidden between curtains, behind the sofa, beyond mirrors, I could sense the mystical family mantra. Spoken out loud from time to time, in English, and regularly sung in Hebrew, in the form of Grace After Meals. "The land you have given us," we chorused in Hebrew after Shabbat dinner. The theme never left the family, nor the family the theme. It was there, whispered, chanted, sung, recited, if not in the house, then on walks by the river under the bridge, winter walks through town. The message of the theme was:

"When Daddy retires we will do it. We will all move to Israel."

§

Mid-morning my mother consults a new doctor on the phone, but this time not for advice about old-age or infirmity. It's about the files again. Green files, blue files, kalamazoo files, every article, every learned journal, every experiment referenced and recorded. But old stuff now. Half the cells he discovered have new names. And anyway, now it's all computerised.

And then there's a phone call. It's Aunt Milly, who came to live here twenty years before any of us did. She will pop in tomorrow with a limp and a stick to see her dying brother. Meanwhile she makes a dire prediction. Tonight there will be more thunder. So much more of it will there be that last night's will be remembered as the calm before. As you're here, she says, tell me what's happening in England now? For years she's said to me on every visit, what a shame you went back, did you really hate it here, or just not like it enough? Were seven years more than sufficient for you? But before I have time to answer she's rung off, gone to listen to the news.

§

This afternoon we sat in the "salon" and he was in the wheelchair. He said, I'll try a little walk. I helped him stand up, and he took a dozen steps. His arm as I held it shook violently with the effort.

Now it's midnight but I can't sleep yet. I'm remembering being woken not by thunder but by thundering. I am very young. Listen. That rumbling, almost a deep growl, or barking. I sit up in bed, wide-eyed, waiting. That noise is the sound of Daddy in the morning running all the way down the stairs then up again. I wait snug in bed, till he canters into our room, slows, opens our curtains. I hear foot-steps, a pause, and a soft click. I still share a room with Tamar who is nine.

"The gas fire is on now, girls! It's safe to get up." And now it's cold, freezing, winter holiday time though we know not to expect presents from Father Christmas. But we have Chanukah, with chocolate coins wrapped in gold and silver paper. Eight whole days of it. And there are so many other days. Christians only have Christmas once a year, he jokes as we walk down the hill to the place I love the most. He holds my hand as we cross the road carefully, then in we go to the Central Library. This is my treat for Shabbat, of which we have fifty-two in a year and each one is lovely.

And now I see myself again as the wide-eyed child, and I am running, my little legs carrying me up and down, through dark blue tunnels, beneath mysterious grey heights, vast mountain ranges of mysteries and wonders. Books, books, books. Words words. English words. I love them. I am the best reader in the family. I read newspapers too, even though I'm only seven. And I am a good girl.

Rabbi, Rabbi

Oh Rabbi, Rabbi, fend my soul for me,
And true savant of this dark nature be.

— Wallace Stevens

The Synagogue called itself Reform, Progressive and Independent. The building was modern, glass and steel. At the back a courtyard was surrounded by walls of ivy, tubbed trees, and flower beds.

The day Tina attended the first of Rabbi Caroline's Shabbat morning services, her mind played tricks on her. It dipped like a bird, taking her diving back through time, to her orthodox childhood when being Jewish was deep and meaningful. For a few years in her youth, the sound of a congregation singing in Hebrew, even when she was perched in the Ladies Gallery looking down, made her feel good. This was before the slow but inexorable drift away from a life where the expressions of values and beliefs centered round the fulfilling of Mitzvot. Caroline sang alto and Tina joined in easily, and on her second Shabbat she had a welcome committee. Two people at the entrance, a woman and a man.

"Hello!" the woman said brightly. She held out an immaculate hand for Tina to shake.

She wore a crimson trouser suit. Her black hair framed a pretty face. The man's handshake was masculine and warmer.

"I'm Charlotte. This is Chris," said the woman, authoritatively. "Chris, this is Tina, our new member."

"Have you been members a long time?" Tina asked innocently, taking them for husband and wife.

"I'm just the caretaker," announced Chris, and she found him instantly likeable.

"Without Chris," Charlotte enthused, "this place would not function."

Six months after she joined the synagogue, it was Friday afternoon, and winter. Tina called in for a purpose. The following day she would be reading Hebrew from the Torah Scroll, in the Shabbat morning service. Caroline waited for her beside the Bimah, the raised wooden platform holding the special desk on which the Scrolls would be opened. Chris stood beside her.

"I was ecstatic," the Rabbi turned to the caretaker, "when this lady here informed me she was able to read from the Torah."

"Wow," he said admiringly, "Where did you learn that?"

"I lived in Israel for four years," Tina told him, "I learned Hebrew." The Israel years. How hard it was to convey to anyone, Jewish or not, the smell of clementine peel thrown on the grass of the National Park in Ashkelon, the shrieks of the black ravens that scooped up the bright orange fragments, then scaled skywards, above the beach, above the ruins left hundreds of years ago by Byzantine generals and crusader zealots. Up and over crystal blue waves, back down again over the crumbling dome that stood silhouetted on the clifftop. This, Alon had told her, was called The Sheik's Tomb. It was a place holy to Muslims. Once upon a time, he whispered in her ear. Story after story, histories real or invented. How he loved her, or said he did. Hebrew is not about religion anymore, he said. It is a language, alive.

"Your knowledge of Hebrew will be a huge asset!" Rabbi Caroline said approvingly. Tina pushed aside memories of Dr. Alon Talberg. His passion for her was fired, she discovered after several months, by pain. His wife had left him, gone to live in Cyprus with their baby. One day out of the blue she came back, and Alon had to tell Tina the truth. That was that. A great love, a great lie.

"We should take the scroll out," the Rabbi said, so Chris moved to the ark to open it.

The four scrolls owned by the Synagogue stood to attention. Chris took one out carefully, and held it while Caroline removed the pomegranate shaped silver finials. They made a tinkling sound as she placed them on the two mini-poles set by the Bimah.

"We call these rimonim," she said to him. Tina knew two meanings of the word. Pomegranate. Hand grenade.

"They're usually silver." Chris handed the Scrolls deferentially to the Rabbi, who eased off the purple velvet covering, laid them down on the reading desk, then carefully undid the ribbon which held the two rolled scrolls together. She turned the Scrolls carefully to the place of tomorrow's reading. Using the silver Yad, a tiny forefinger pointing, she gently touched the words. Tina leaned forward to get a clear look.

Hebrew words were inked on the parchment, in lines and columns. A dense, condensed record of history. Genesis to Deuteronomy. Where did the music, the tropes she knew well, come from? From unknown composers of her past. What was the content? Lists of names. God said to Moses, Moses said to the people, tribes came and went. Standards were set, of a kind. The tracks of her identity laid down mysteriously in words on parchment. History, laws, prophets. And what, Tina asked herself, if none of the people in this scroll even existed? It is still the history of who I am. Somebody must have written the stories. And they, real or fiction, have followed me to where I am today.

With Chris's help, Caroline rolled and re-covered the scroll. He carried it carefully back to the ark, hung a ribbon over it, to mark it for tomorrow's service. Then he stood back, and gazed at the row of scrolls, upright with their silver accoutrements.

"Sometimes, when it's quiet, I open the Ark and use these as objects of meditation." He spoke reverentially. "Do you think I'm a bit mad?"

"Not at all," Tina said. Unconventional, perhaps. By now she had learned that he was an English teacher. He was also responsible for the cornucopia of colours in the garden, spring summer and autumn. He occupied a studio flat at the back of the building.

Tina was a social worker, not yet thirty. Through clients' troubled histories she cast her caring eye over the world, or parts of it. She was at peace. The turbulent time with Alon in Israel was in the past. She would have liked to have a new partner, but otherwise life was fine.

Some weeks later, Charlotte phoned her. "We have a place available on the Synagogue Council," she said, "Might you be interested?"

For the first time in her life Tina gave thought to the fact that a Synagogue is more than a conceptual pathway. It is an institution. It requires committees with white tables and people to sit at them.

"How long have you been chair for?" she asked Charlotte.

"Nine years. I was a young graduate when I started. Management and Business Studies." Tina regretted that a rabbi's line manager should be so down-to-earth. Management and Business? Charlotte wore grey tinted glasses matched with metal-grey droop earrings.

"I'm not sure a Synagogue council is where I want to be," Tina said truthfully. Those terms - management, business - made her uneasy. Jew equals business and all that. What was wrong with her? Synagogues have to be run somehow.

§

Every time Tina saw Chris, she pictured him opening the ark and meditating in front of the scrolls. Correction. Occasionally she imagined him doing that but more often she imagined other scenarios. The best one: she was locked in the Synagogue; or perhaps she just turned up there. It was dark. In a corner, in shadows, she noticed him and he noticed her. If you were a writer, he would ask her, what would you write about?

Jewish life, she would reply. The essence of it. No writer gets to the essence of it. They would talk. Then he would kiss her. The touch of his lips would be subtle, hot and not at all casual.

A month later, Rabbi Caroline phoned, and asked Tina to call in to discuss something. She received Tina in her study. She sat at her office furniture desk, surrounded by DIY shelving, books in English and Hebrew stacked at hair-raising angles.

"I wanted to talk to you about Chris. With his permission, I can tell you he has decided to convert. And we're looking for someone to teach him Hebrew."

"I'll do it," Tina said.

"He's a gentle soul," said Caroline, "quite spiritual. Although I ought to say, spiritual is one of those words. I never get what it means. I hope you're not offended. Many people convert because of another person, a relationship. Chris, it appears is doing it because he believes he was meant to be Jewish. Something rather lovely about it, if you ask me."

Tina had a sense of history, culture and community. She spoke and read Hebrew and loved music and poetry. She contemplated telling Rabbi Caroline that she no longer believed in God, but stopped herself on the grounds that this was not her journey, it was his. No reason why she couldn't be his guide to Hebrew, and to a kind of Jewish life.

They met for lessons in his studio flat behind the Synagogue hall. Tina sat on Chris's charcoal grey sofa. "I'm not the best person," she said modestly, "to educate you in matters religious."

"But the Rabbi says you'll be a great Hebrew teacher."

"Hebrew is two different languages. On the one hand it's the language we pray in - or try to! As such, it represents what some people believe is a connection between a real God, and how we live, not to mention the real, actual land of Israel. But for other people it is nothing but a language. A culture and a history yes – but that is definitely all."

"OK," he replied carefully.

"I'm not saying I have reservations about teaching you. I don't." On the contrary. She felt drawn to this man. They had known each other before - the idea came to her – in a previous incarnation. Not that she believed in reincarnation. It was three years since she had split up with Alon, left Israel.

"Let's not talk it to death," Chris suggested. "I'll start by learning to read."

"This sofa is comfortable." Something material and straightforward.

"It came from my mother's house, in Wales. When I was a child, Dad told me stories on it. When he died Mum had it re-covered." She imagined Chris a child beside her, looking up, wanting a story. It came to her with a startling ache - if she was ever going to have children, they would have to be his. Meanwhile he smiled and said, "I never thought I would convert, you know, not in a hundred years. Both my parents were staunch believers in humanism. Nothing else."

"I suppose I'm a humanist. A Jewish humanist."

"They were straightforward atheists."

Tina reached out her hand, he took it and held it briefly, lightly.

"I'm not sure this was what the Rabbi had in mind," he moved a little, "when she asked if I'd like to learn with you." Tina's face glowed.

"Sorry."

"Don't be sorry. I'm not. But to be honest," he spoke gently and she felt cherished, cared for, "so much is changing in my life now, it wouldn't be fair for me to get involved. Even with someone I really like." He said "really like" with conviction.

"Of course."

Then he kissed her, and that lasted seven seconds.

§

"What started you on the road to becoming Jewish?"

"A history teacher I knew. She said one day, the reason why schools teach about the Holocaust but never teach about genocides anywhere else is this: Jews control the media. Fact. How do they do this? I asked her. Easy, she said. They own all the banks."

This conversation, which happened during their third lesson, took Tina to a place she really did not like. That place where you had to be super alert to rising antisemitism, if it was indeed rising. She had neither the time nor patience to go there.

"The following week," said Chris, "there was a flare up on the Gaza Israel border. This same woman phoned me and screamed. Bloody Israel is bombing the hell out of defenceless civilians. That makes them far worse than Nazis. That is why we have antisemitism!" He'd heard enough. He resolved to explore the Jewish world thoughtfully, and if possible to become part of it.

§

"Come in," the Rabbi pushed a mug of tea to one side, in her untidy office.

"I just wanted a word about something. Nothing major. But. You asked me to teach Chris."

"Is there a problem? He seems to be learning Hebrew at twice the rate everyone else does. How are you doing it?"

"It isn't me. He wants to learn, that's all."

"So what's the problem?"

"I feel less than entirely honest."

"Because you struggle with belief? You know, no rabbi expects another Jew to make regular declarations of faith. You may think, believe, whatever you like. I can show you verses from the Talmud."

"Thank you. That's reassuring. We do get on well."

"For some reason you are being too conscientious. He'll decide what to make of the Hebrew."

"I do enjoy teaching him." The seven second kiss. The hours of pleasure . . . remembering it. She felt herself blushing. Rabbi Caroline put up a hand, bent her head forward, and smiled at the table.

"A little crush, is it? There is no need for you to tell me about your relationship – unless you feel it could damage or be damaged by your lessons. He thinks highly of you. You think well of him. So far all good."

"I enjoy teaching him. No point over-analysing it, then. Thank you."

"You reinforce my impression that you are considerate and perceptive. Kol Hakavod!" A Hebrew phrase - well done.

Tina left the room knowing herself to be a good actress. Truth was, she was passionately in love. His symmetrical face, steady stare, the fair hair that fell forward over his pale blue eyes, and the dimples. He must have been a cherubic looking child. She was not pretty herself, the mirror told her, but she could look lively and animated, and that would have to be enough for him. Her face was inadequate, rather thin, the mirror added. Hopefully their children would look like him.

§

Next lesson, he surprised her.

"I'm assisting Rabbi Caroline at a funeral," he said. "Helping mourners when they get to the cemetery; handing out prayer books. I would like to be able to read the funeral service."

"Most people recite the Hebrew without under-standing it," Tina said, "and then they read the English."

"Show me both," he said. So there she was, sit-ting at his small table, heads close, as he read the Hebrew. When he came to the part "shelter him/her under the shadow of your wings," he put the book to one side.

"This is beautiful," he said.

"It's poetic, isn't it?" she agreed. "Real poetry."

"For some it is more than that," he said gently.

At the following lesson Tina showed Chris some Hebrew newspapers online. He was able to spell out headlines. "Demonstration in Tel Aviv. Thousands dance and sing." So she told him more about Alon Talberg.

"He was an Israeli doctor. He was in an organi-zation called Physicians for Human Rights. Radical, political. He was bitterly against the occupation, of course."

"The settler movement, you mean."

"Yes. All of that. Wanting Israel to keep the occupied West Bank, thinking they have a God-given right, you know. Alon was passionately against all that." Chris turned his head and gazed out of the window. Perhaps she shouldn't have mentioned her old lover. She assumed Chris was bored. She won-dered what the tribulations of her secular Israel really meant to him.

"God-given right," Chris repeated quietly. "That phrase is often used to depict something one has to disapprove of. But from what we have been reading, from what you have taught me to read, what God has given us ought to be celebrated – not disparaged. Is there no positive way of describing what we have been given?" His earnest stare, his even teeth. Except one, the one, just to the right, protruding slightly. It gave his smile more character.

"I'm not sure what you mean."

"I mean, and it's in all the prayers I am learning to read, that God really has given us something."

I am thinking about sex, and you are talking about God, she thought, and imagined that years from now, when they were old, she would confess just how she felt on this particular evening which had a peculiar feel to it. A sense of imminence. She felt it. They were next to each other, inches between them. He put out his arm as if to embrace her, but instead looped it over the back of the chair.

"I've been making plans, Tina, and I need to talk to you about them. You must be aware how much your teaching means to me."

"Nice of you to say." He stood up, moved away suddenly, and posed with his back to the prints on the wall. One print of Picasso bulls, the other a Chagall. The one of the man and woman flying through the air. He looked down at her. "I've been on the verge of telling you for a while. I am going away for at least a year."

"Where are you going?"

"No! First ask why I am going!" Pause. "Because of you. These last few months you have been a ray of light that shone on my life and illuminated it."

I am not going to cry, Tina said to herself, tears welling.

"You brought so much to life for me, you showed me the beauty of Hebrew and of Jewish life. And Caroline, of course supported me too. You have both been wonderful. But . . ."

"What?"

"You're really not aware of what has been happening to me . . . ?"

"I could tell there was something," Tina managed to say.

"This feels like a confession, but it shouldn't be. I don't feel I have done anything wrong. From the outset, I have been studying with others, too. One of the reasons I learned so fast. I don't want to make comparisons. No. Let me be honest - you deserve honesty. I have been making comparisons. I have been exploring Judaism, and I have come to the conclusion that to be a full-blown sincere convert, I have to do it in the traditional way – I mean, learn to live the whole life, not just half of it."

She felt sick.

"I've been learning with a rabbi from the other synagogue. Rabbi Gelberman."

"Obviously, your decision. Your choice. I did not see this coming, actually. I saw your journey as a journey into the Progressive Jewish world. But – hey, whatever you do. Good luck!"

"Thanks. I'm going to Jerusalem, for a year. The fact that it means this much to me, that I am quivering with excitement about being there – I have you to thank for it. Only one thing makes me sad."

The Kiss, surely?

"It's the way that you do love Hebrew - up to a point, but then you dismiss its depth, its histories, the fact that it is the language of God. I don't mean literally. But to me it does have holiness in it. Or an aspiration at least. I am so sorry that for you it's just like . . . any other language."

"We kissed" was the worst thing to say. Her tears set off like skiers let loose on a slope of sheer ice and her body was cold.

"I am genuinely sorry. That was wrong of me. But at least we learned from it. I hope we will always be friends."

§

"Come in!"

One year later. For the first time since joining the synagogue, Tina was invited to Friday night dinner at Rabbi Caroline's. The Rabbi opened the door and said Welcome, Shabbat Shalom!

In this kitchen Tina's mind dipped once more like a bird into memory. Caroline leaned over to adjust the dial on a large stainless steel urn. What, in childhood, Tina had known as a Shabbos Kettle.

"I didn't buy it specifically for Chris," Caroline laughed. "It's been in my loft for decades! But in his honour, for tonight." The kitchen table was covered in a paper cloth. The crockery, ready in advance of the meal, was plastic, throwaway. "Chris was here this afternoon! We went through everything. Tonight I am more kosher than kosher. He's given it the go-ahead, and I must tell you I appreciate his broadmindedness. Not many Orthodox converts would be prepared to eat in the house of a Reform rabbi. He always was an exceptional person, your Christopher. I've invited Charlotte, too. He`ll be late, by the way. He's at Rabbi Gelberman's shul for the Friday night service, and will then walk here. And may I say, hats off to Rabbi G. Not many Orthodox rabbis would co-teach someone already learning in a Reform context."

The fulfilling of Mitzvot, the fulfilling of Mitzvot. The phrase came back to her. The melody from a symphonic first movement hauntingly returning in the finale. The life she had walked away from. The intricate web of commandments which, if you observed them connected you to God, encircling you, protecting you, defining you, and separating you, day by day, always. Now Chris was choosing to live that way. First thing in the morning he would wash his hands, cover his head, say morning blessings. Next thing, wind the Tefillin – the phylacteries - round his arm, say morning prayers. Later in the day, pray again. And marriage? How often had she shared that she was the new kind of Jew? Shaky on belief, casual in observance, and open, above all open, to the whole wide world – not separated from it. And he, he to her was that world. And she had opened to him. Did he ever like her, let alone love her? Had she seen this coming?

No.

And here it was at last, and here they were. Shabbat Night. Chris arrived looking slim and sunburnt. Charlotte arrived, and presented Caroline with a box of chocolates with Hebrew writing on it. Chris handed Tina Collected Poems by Wallace Stevens.

"Thank you so much," Tina said. The excitement of having him back, and near her was more than she could bear.

After dinner, Chris announced out of the blue that he wanted to sing Shir Hamaalot, something Tina hadn't done since childhood. "Grace After Meals," The Rabbi said helpfully to Charlotte. "It begins with a psalm," she added.

When Chris began to sing, in Hebrew, Tina saw how he put trust in the melody, the words. His singing sounded heartfelt, and was pitch-perfect in tune. Why wouldn't he look at her?

At the end, because Charlotte knew no Hebrew at all, Rabbi Caroline read the translation.

When the Lord returned the captives of Zion, we were like people in a dream. Then was our mouth filled with laughter, and our tongue with exultation: then said they among the nations, The Lord has done great things for them. The Lord has done great things for us; so we rejoiced! Bring back our captives, O Lord, as the streams in the south. They that sow in tears shall reap in joy.

"I'm staying with a family in Jerusalem," said Chris, "and they always sing at the table on Shabbat." Tina's hands rested on Rabbi Caroline's table. It felt soft, about to give way. He smiled at her at last, optimistically, then he took a photograph out of his pocket, and made her stare at it. A father, bearded, a kippah on his head, a mother with a long skirt, and two daughters. He pointed to the pretty one. "This is Avital."

"Do tell us about her," Rabbi Caroline murmured.

"She's a nurse," he said. "Incredibly caring." The people at the table moved round and round, each one smiling, like dream figures. Yes, this was a dream. In a different reality Chris would be sitting here, kippah on his head maybe, comfortable now with the Hebrew she had taught him, and he would be relaxing into her moderate way of life and loving her. Loving her to the end of her days. Instead, what was he doing?

"I am going to complete my conversion in the orthodox way," he asserted gently, "it's something I know I need to do. But I can never say thank you enough to you guys, especially to you, Tina. And you Rabbi Caroline. Always."

"Will you live permanently in Israel?" the Rabbi asked.

"There is a small settlement called Brachot. Blessings! Avital has a flat there, for the first year. After that we'll see. Please wish me luck!" Chris looked at Tina hopefully. How dare he?

"Occupied land, Chris," she spoke coldly, trying not to sound aggressive, feeling both responsible and heartbroken – not to mention angry.

"It was in the words," he said to her. "You showed me. The history, the ideas, and they took me to other places. There was always God in my journey. I followed God that's all. I hate to think you disapprove."

"I don't disapprove of people believing in God. But I hate to think my teaching led you to want to be in a settlement in the West Bank. Do you remember my telling you about a good friend of mine, Dr Alon Talberg, who worked for Physicians for Human Rights?"

I loved someone before you, and I will love someone else now you have deserted me.

"I will always be your grateful friend, Tina. I told Avital everything about us."

"If you need me to spell it out, life on the West Bank is unjust and cruel to two million Palestinians."

"Avital is an oncology nurse," he said carefully. Yes, he'd expected this conversation. "Half her patients, half her colleagues are Palestinians, and grateful. She loves them. They love her. She is kind and sincere, and respects everyone."

Rabbi Caroline looked sad and troubled. "I believe and will continue to believe that there is room for dialogue between you both," she said gently, adding hopefully, "between us all, really."

"Of course!" Chris agreed, "Of course there is! But I must be getting on now. Quite a walk back to the Gelbermans." He stood up, and actually backed away from the three women, who all stood up too. Each one followed him to the front door, each with a reason to say goodbye nicely.

"Thank you to all of you," he clasped his hands together as he spoke, and Tina knew this was to protect himself, lest he put out a hand and touch one of them. He would never touch a woman again, apart from Avital, and their daughters if they were to have any.

She stood at the open door to watch him leave. Above her there were clouds, and an unstable looking moon lit up the night. It was a moment, surely, when a mind like hers ought to be able to conjure something, some sense of meaning, from this desolate farewell to a man whose path she herself had partly carved? Words flowed past her in the dark, not quite visible. She couldn't reach out, catch them, find what it was she needed to say, to think, in this moment of loss that she would never ever forget.

Camping Maybe

"Dear Patricia, thank you for sending us Camping Maybe. We found it well-written and amusing. Is it your intention to produce the play? We were wondering what your thoughts are. Perhaps come and have chat. Suggest speak to set up meeting? Don Kenning. Artistic Director. Purple Rug Theatre."

Ten years of writing plays, and at last this. Stay calm my soul, all will be well. I am forty-two, there is everything to play for.

§

Heart palpitating, Pat googled Don Kenning. "This man is a talent spotter. Producers flock to his small venue, look vaguely for a purple rug, then sit down to enjoy play after play that his discerning team of readers have unearthed for the theatre-loving literati of London." This from an English language tour guide – previously an actor – in Berlin.

When he wrote "Suggest speak to set up meeting," Pat assumed Kenning would phone her. So she let a month pass, and another. Then she called him. Then she called him again. The first time, no reply, the second time: "Don here. Leave message. I'll get back to you."

"Hi this is Patricia Blake. You sent me an email about my play, Camping Maybe, and suggested we might speak. A few weeks ago? I would really like to meet up, which is what you suggested. I was delighted you liked the play. I'm happy to come over. Let me know. Look forward to hearing from you."

A frustrating fortnight later, Pat stood in the lift at the tube station, and with each metre it rose, her spirits rose too. Two more phone messages and he still hadn't replied - but perhaps he'd given her a wrong number. Or he'd been ill. Or he was away. Or, most likely, he was busy directing a current production. That was why she had come. The Purple Rug was on the main road, yards from the tube. The play she was going to see was a revival of something from the nineteen-sixties.

The pub theatre was at the top of three flights of stairs. There was neither handrail nor carpeting on the tortuously twisting top flight. A low door, curtained, and the box office. A tiny space, a man behind a desk. She recognized Don Kenning from his website.

"Hello. I'm Patricia Blake. I wrote Camping Maybe."

"Oh! Hi. Lovely to meet you at last. Great that you have come! Um." He looked down vaguely at his desk – strewn with pieces of paper. He picked one up. "Yes. It was a real shame you missed our meeting."

"What meeting?"

"Wednesday morning. We were supposed to meet, weren't we? I had it written down somewhere. Yes. Here. We spoke and you were coming over."

"Look, I'm sorry," she said, "but we haven't spoken – maybe it was someone else." Cool as anything, he screwed up the piece of paper and threw it down. Destroying the evidence, she thought. He's a liar.

"Never mind, glad you're here. We did enjoy your play. I like the fact that it has two characters over the age of forty. My old friends from drama school are queueing to audition." So he was thinking of putting it on.

"Could we fix a different date, please? So I can come in and talk? I would like to know how it all works."

"Tell you what – you don't direct, do you? I thought not. Let me show the play to one or two people. A play like this cries out for a good director. And we'll discuss a budget of some kind. I'll get back to you in a week or two."

§

Five months later she was woken in the night. Her husband was asleep beside her. She heard whispering from downstairs. She sat up carefully, swung her legs, walked, put on her maroon dressing-gown. She went downstairs to the kitchen. They were waiting for her, sitting at the table. Both of them - Clare and Justin. Clare and Justin, in conversation with each other. With a thrill, Pat saw and heard the characters she had created. Come to life! In the flesh!

She saw them, and heard them. The real thing, here at her kitchen table.

"Shit. If I had known it would be like this – I would not have said what I said on that day in that bar, and I certainly wouldn't have done what I did." Clare sounded apologetic.

"Blaming yourself is unhelpful." Justin, too, spoke as she had always imagined, in a deep-throated way. He was taller than she'd envisaged, and more good-looking. His hair was dark and at the front there was a streak of white - a sign of something. Who were these people?

"Who are you?" Pat whispered, to the couple, who were strangers yet darkly known.

"Precisely what we are trying to work out," said Clare snidely. Pat grinned to herself. Clare had said exactly what she herself might have said. Pat felt a rising sense of panic, and withdrew. She turned her back, and shuddered at a small sound. Was that one of them opening the cutlery drawer, taking out a knife? Was it Justin, picking up his viola? Was he carrying the viola from scene three? She left the kitchen and banged the door behind her. She raced upstairs in the dark, and threw herself back in bed, making sure to nudge and wake Andrew. He turned towards her and put out a casual arm.

"I had an incredible dream," she whispered. He resumed snoring. "I went down to the kitchen and I found them there, both of them. The people in my play. Clare and Justin!"

A year and eight months later – Pat found herself sitting in row two of the empty Purple Rug, watching at long last the first rehearsal of Camping Maybe. The stage was positioned so the audience would sit on three sides. Thrust Staging, they called it. Opposite Pat sat Valerie the director, who had emerged from her hermit's life on Dartmoor to direct (Don Kenning had said) one more play before dying. She was in her late sixties. She had cancelled what should have been the first rehearsal, Monday's, and also the second, Tuesday's. Today was Wednesday. Two days of rehearsing lost already, out of the total of fifteen (Monday to Friday over three weeks).

Behind her, keeping quiet for the moment, sat the real Clare and the real Justin. Laugh at them, Andrew had advised. Go with the flow. They are figments of your imagination, nothing more! But Pat knew otherwise. They were real. Whatever reality was, they had earned theirs. Through her, maybe, but they had earned it.

The email for today had said Wednesday ten am to five thirty but actually they started after eleven, and at four o'clock Valerie began yawning and said OK enough for today. But the play had finally started to come to life.

The actors playing Clare and Justin slung their bags over their shoulders, waved goodbye to playwright and director, and exited. The real Clare and Justin watched them leave curiously.

Then the real Justin gazed critically after Colin, his actor, and complained, "Why get someone in his forties to play me, when I am thirty-eight?"

Valerie came to sit beside Pat, and the two of them gazed at the empty theatre where scenes had been played out. Director and playwright side by side in the small black box of an empty fringe venue. Then Valerie began to tell her story.

§

When Don Kenning wrote asking her to direct Camping Maybe, she couldn't remember who he was. Ten years since she'd seen him. She had given up directing years ago. But he said she would be the best person for this play.

Valerie lived high up on Dartmoor. Beyond her hill there was bog. The bog played host to sedges of all shapes and sizes, and the greens browns and reds did her head in, particularly in summer, and sometimes made her wish her life was different, and that she'd been an artist. In June, came flowering cotton grass. Gorgeous. Delicate. And below her the moors turned into seas of yellow and purple - heathers and gorse in flower. She was lucky, people said to have these views.

"And don't get me started on orchids. Just don't." What is the play about, she asked Don but she had already said yes. It was assumed the fee would be minimal. She was, to be honest, in a lonely patch. Not that loneliness on its own (ha ha) was ever the thing to complain about. It's a quality of being human.

Valerie got herself to London and found a room near The Purple Rug, with a landlady called Vi. Vi had a black cat and made Valerie mushrooms on white toast for breakfast, cauliflower cheese at night. She was merry and bright but something about her made Valerie behave irresponsibly. When she came in late, she was supposed to attach the safety chain to the door, after closing it. Two nights running she didn't, just didn't. No idea why.

Valerie came to The Purple Rug committed to doing her best. By now she had read through the play, Camping Maybe. In the play Clare was married to viola player Justin, and then Justin's old friend Solomon turned up – off stage - needing money and sex. Clare knew he was an unreliable man but fancied him more than she did Justin, who was decent and straightforward. Both Clare and Justin became fascinated by their friend Solomon's unreliability and minor crimes. So they made a plan to go camping together in France. Separate tents, they said. Provence, and they would go by Eurostar. A clear lack of self-awareness in both Clare and Justin, and their inability to talk openly to each other, these were the characteristics that gave the play its punch.

On day four of rehearsals (the Thursday of the first week) Valerie came early, to prepare for her second day of directing for the first time in years. She was surprised to find the black box rehearsal space still dark, but there was the shape of a man sitting on the floor.

"Hi," said actor Colin, "I'm a bit early. I was about to do warm-ups." Within seconds this seriously wacky director felt a mystical pull on her heart – her artistic never-to-be-satisfied heart, and within minutes she became convinced beyond doubt that he felt a pull too. The actor was thirty-eight. Character Justin was forty. Valerie was sixty-eight. What did age matter? Inwardly she thanked Don Kenning who had kindly sourced the cast.

Colin sat cross legged, meditating.

"Tell me about yourself, Colin," Valerie suggested sweetly. "Have you got a girlfriend?"

"Yes. My partner lives in Kent. We're expecting a baby in the new year."

But those were just words. For Valerie, his stilness, his focus, his calm, pierced her soul. When their eyes met, something instant, ancient, overwhelmed her. Emma, the actress playing Clare arrived, and then Pat the playwright. Colin raised an arm slightly, to greet them both, but Valerie interpreted his greeting personally. She saw it as a salute from afar to her, his Twin Flame. The universe had brought them together. What a gift.

§

Pat deduced pretty quickly that the director of her play was useless. Valerie was permanently blearyeyed, and mainly wanted to grumble about Vi, her landlady. Then she asked Pat, "Stand me a bacon sandwich for lunch? The actors might appreciate sandwiches too."

Don Kenning popped in, to show them where the kettle was – on the draining board of a sink that was a hundred years old in the theatre's only dressing-room. This old pub had once been a large house. Up here were the servants' quarters. The kettle didn't work, so next day Pat brought the spare kettle from home.

But the following morning, Friday, kettles and sandwiches were the least of Pat's problems. After a suffocating tube journey, she arrived at The Purple Rug to find it locked. At the front of the building, in what had once been a small garden, there were old benches and tables. At one table sat Valerie, leaning studiously over a large notepad. Relieved, Pat thought Valerie was at last connecting with the play and making notes, sketching ideas for staging, blocking, or whatever. Colin who played Justin and Emma in the part of Clare sat at the next table. Emma looked bored, and Colin uneasy. Valerie said, quietly but urgently, "Don't move, Colin or I'll have to start again." Then she noticed playwright Pat. "Hi," she said, "the place wasn't open so we sat ourselves down. I'm indulging my other skill. Look. Is it a likeness?" She held up a charcoal portrait of Colin - naked.

"Lucky it isn't raining." Pat tried to sound cheerful, and not to feel embarrassed.

"You've got a key I suppose," Valerie said hopefully.

"No. I assumed you had one."

"Why would I have one? I'm just the fucking director."

Worse than this were the miserable looks on the faces of the real Clare and Justin, who Pat noticed now, hunched over the far table, in the shadow of a dead privet hedge. Justin's arm was looped loosely over his beloved viola case. All waited – the real and the unreal. It was an hour and a half since Pat had left home. If someone like Don Kenning didn't come soon and open The Purple Rug, she knew beyond doubt that she would wet herself.

Week Two arrived. This week has to be different, Pat said to herself, standing on the platform waiting for the tube. She was no longer on cloud nine, no longer believing either in her skills as a playwright or the reliability of Don Kenning.

The real Clare and Justin insisted on travelling with her on the Northern Line. When the sounds of underground travel got to their loudest, they smiled comfortingly to calm her. She wondered whether they might talk out loud, take advantage of the shrieking growls of the train, but they didn't. But as they walked alongside her towards The Purple Rug, Justin spoke.

"That actor Colin is too young to play me, and he knows it. The director can't take her eyes off him. Given half a chance, she wouldn't take her hands off him either. Bloody disgusting."

"OK guys," Valerie welcomed the two she could see, and Pat the writer, and ignored the two she couldn't.

"So. A word about Week Two. On Wednesday I won't be able to get here until two o'clock. If you like, if Pat can get here with the key, you can come in the morning and do line runs."

"Val," said the playwright urgently, "we missed two days rehearsing last week. I'm nervous. How long does it normally take to rehearse a play?"

"I'm doing this for virtually nothing," said Valerie coldly, "doing Don Kenning a favour. I have a doctor's appointment on Wednesday. If it's a choice between my health and your play, I'm afraid health must win."

Emma playing Clare announced she would like Wednesday afternoon off also. A friend was recently bereaved. But she assured them she would be off the book by Friday.

"So - if you're not here Wednesday afternoon," Valerie said to Emma, "and I'm not here in the morning, I suggest we write Wednesday off. Agreed?"

"No, please!" Pat protested, desperate to protect her play, "There won't be enough rehearsal time. There just won't."

"Don't worry," said Valerie, "It'll be all right on the night. There's a reason why they say it."

At least, on this day, the first day of the second week, they did a complete read through of the play, but when Valerie offered feedback to the actors she was unnecessarily curt with Emma; hostile, almost.

"I honestly believe," said Emma defensively, "that Clare loves Justin. It's just that she loves Solomon too. Basically they all love each other. That is the source of the lovely tension in this gorgeous piece."

Valerie looked stony-faced and disapproving. Then she snapped at poor Emma playing Clare. Colin playing Justin looked surprised.

"As director," Valerie ordered, "I am supposed to have a view, and indeed I do have one. The character we never see in this play, Solomon, is basically a piece of shit, and the audience needs to know that. Justin on the other hand has all the qualities." She smiled tenderly at Colin playing Justin.

"Sorry . . ." Writers were not supposed to interfere but Pat couldn't help herself. "But I agree with Emma. I would say Clare loves both of them. If the play has a point, that's it. I ought to know. I wrote it."

The real Justin nodded approval, and the real Clare reached out to him, and now they posed as if for a photograph. Pat smiled in their direction. They reminded her of a statue in an art gallery in Florence. A woman with a man.

"By the way," Valerie added heavily, "I'm cutting the stuff about the viola. We don't need extra props in the play."

"But Justin holds on to the viola for the whole of scene three," Pat argued stubbornly, trying to sound authoritative. After all – she had written this play, not the director. "His integrity as a musician, his integrity as a man. Connected."

"Sorry," said Valerie stubbornly. "That's not what I get from the script. That's why I say no viola. That is a directorial decision," she added in a domineering tone. Pat trembled, afraid of bringing the whole production crashing down. She sat tensely then till the end of the rehearsal. The email had said eleven till five thirty, but at four o'clock Valerie yawned and said might as well call it a day.

§

On the opening night Pat stood for an hour outside The Purple Rug clutching the handful of flyers that Andrew had prepared. Cheap looking A4 sheets folded in two. A woman took one, but walked on without reading it. Pat watched the woman screw it up and toss it in the gutter.

Now it was seven twenty and the show was to begin at half-past. Pat hurried upstairs, praying there would be more than five people in the audience. As she climbed she imagined herself in the Lake District, climbing a mountain, getting to the top. After the last twist of staircase she turned and saw Don Kenning sitting at his shabby little desk, "doing box office."

"Hello!" She hoped he might be as excited as she was about her opening night, but he didn't look her in the eye. Instead, he reached out for an envelope, a sealed one, and handed it to her.

"Hi," he said.

"Not a huge audience," she said, determined to stay cheerful.

"Regarding the money side," Don flapped the envelope at her like a fan, till she took it, "we'll sort it out next week. We're not charging you for the theatre. But I agreed with Valerie that the actors will need something from the production company."

"What production company?" Pat stared at this man, whose dark eyes and pale face made him look phantom-like.

"I have no idea. That's what Valerie told them. I think it's really just a modest fee. Something for each week. Plus expenses. Surely you have discussed her director's fee."

"No actually."

"You don't expect a director to come to London for a few weeks, not to mention the actors' expenses... Look – read this later and see what you think. We'll get it sorted. For tonight – break a leg. Hope it goes well."

There really were five people in the audience. One was Andrew, on the front row. One, Valerie in the back row. In the second row there were three strangers. The real Clare and Justin were there of course, but no one saw them apart from Pat.

She sat rigid, clutching the sealed envelope which felt alarmingly thick. Invoices from everyone, he'd said. How dare he? How dare they? What an idiot she was. She looked at her innocent husband. How incredibly stupid of him to be proud of her – they weren't very rich at all.

§

The lights faded, and anything that had gone before ceased to matter. Her play rose from the earth, or at least the stage, and there was life in it. The audience of five melted into the dark, swirled, reconfigured, and lo, turned itself into an audience of fifty-five. Magic.

And then, at last, they began to talk, Clare and Justin, as represented by Emma and Colin. But talk they did, and love they did, and laugh they did and come to life they did. And the real Clare and Justin were pretty gripped too, and leaned in, in fascination.

The audience of three that had become fifty-five laughed out loud, and one wiped her eyes in the scene where the couple lay flat on their backs looking up at the stars. And it happened, even in this tiny theatre, that the roof came off, it rose up high, and there were stars, real stars up above, and there was the actual sound of a nearby waterfall. You could hear it. And Pat felt moved, to hear her own words, and relive her own scenarios. And she said this to herself: even if this never happens again, it will have been worth it.

§

Between the end of the play and the applause, the magic faded. The audience shrank back to five. Not wanting to break the spell, fulfilled in a way she imagined might never happen to her again, Pat set off downstairs, not thinking to stay and speak with Valerie or the actors.

She went carelessly down the stairs, hardly holding the bannister, but when with a jolt she found herself almost tripping, she grabbed at it to steady herself. She had been close to tumbling headfirst. Her head swam. She had a sense of unreality.

Look, it is now time, she told herself to calm down, return to normal life, get on with things. She turned to look behind her, and spoke to one of the three strangers in the audience. A young man, with an old-fashioned peaked cap.

"Take care," she warned. "Take care on the stairs. Carefully, she descended to the ground floor. The staircase ended in a small vestibule, in which an antique coatrack held coats and jackets. On a cracked wooden table, half hidden by coats, she saw a viola case, half open, and in it, the real Justin's viola. She smiled, and said to herself: so he did bring it, but he left it here; soon he'll pass by and pick it up. Yes, she thought to herself - Justin was real. The viola was real. Whatever real means. She put out a hand to feel its shiny wood, and traced with her fingers across the strings. Absolutely no question.

Granny Malin's Message

Keep your tongue from evil, and your lips from speaking deceit.

Psalm 34

I came out of my bedroom. This was opposite the door to our grandmother's room. Granny Malin wasn't in residence at the time. During my teenage years she moved between our home, and the home of my father's sad sister Pearl. Pearl was often miserable, I was told. In the dark moods of my adolescence, I sulked, ate too much and didn't clean my nails. Then my father would look at me with contempt, mixed with sorrowful paternal love, and warn me, "You're growing up to be like Pearl."

That morning, sun streamed through the skylight onto the mottled red carpet. My idea became words. Perhaps I'll grow up to be a writer! And from that moment I knew I had to keep an eye permanently open, looking for things to write about.

Our neighbours, Karl and Suzi Elterman were particularly close to my grandmother. Suzi came by on the days Granny Malin arrived, every time. My mother said Suzi came to be shouted at. Granny Malin was the only person in the world she was prepared to be disciplined by.

"Suzi! You have been smoking again!"

"Sorry, Granny,"

"Suzi, you need a haircut!"

"Of course! I will get one. Today!"

I understood why Suzi needed to borrow my grandmother. The Eltermans had no parents, apparently, or none that I ever saw or heard about. I thought they were amazing. My parents didn't need to tell me that they were clever. Off all scales. The most intelligent people I would ever come across. In their house, two whole walls were built out of books alone. Their only child, Oliver, was growing up to be brilliant too. They gave him extra coaching at almost everything because he was top of the class at everything. Professor Karl explained this to me once over the garden wall.

"There are two reasons," he said," for giving a child extra tutoring. One is if he is bad at something. The other – if he is good at it. Don't you agree?" By a previously unheard of arrangement, Oliver was invited to attend Oxford and Cambridge at the same time. There was a feature about this in The Times.

Granny Malin, my father's mother, darned socks and spun yarns. There was a style of resolute irony in her way of talking. Also, she had a jokey obsession with the socks. Perhaps she spent too much time darning. Gazing at rows of them on the kitchen pulley, she would flick one off, her thick hands hovering, then scan the wooden poles earnestly.

"Now," she would ask, in an almost Kantian-analytic tone, "where . . . is its mate?"

And stories?

"The two most wonderful things," she told me, "are these. First, stories. Long stories, in any language you like!"

"And the second thing?" I asked.

"Apples. English coxes. Only coxes."

On the day I decided to be a writer, Granny Malin was at Pearl's in cloudy Lancashire. A year later, when I was sixteen, she came back to us. She seemed less strong than I remembered, and on her first evening, I listened carefully to the arrangements my parents put in place. If Granny woke in the night feeling ill, she had to knock with her stick.

A week later I was woken at three in the morning by the thudding of that stick on the wall between her room and our parents" room. The thuds were insistent but weak.

"Granny's passed away," my father said gently to me, hours later, as I stood on the landing, too scared to be in the room. Then, later that morning, Suzi Elterman came in and surprised me. She shrugged, gave only a half-sad smile, and looked ludicrously relaxed.

"Don't grieve too much," she instructed me. "Your Granny lived here with all of you in comfort and safety. It is sad that she died, but not tragic. Do you understand me? There is oblivion for her now – and that is all." She shrugged, in her Czechoslovakian way.

My mother was furious with Suzi for talking this way to me, when I was having my first close experience of death. My father suggested we have nothing more to do with them. But mother said that wouldn't work. She reminded us that their ideas were different to ours. They had agreed, for example that if one of them was dying the other certainly would not sit around grieving.

Some time later, I wandered into Granny's empty room to find my mother sitting on the old double bed, wiping her eyes.

"Are you missing her?" I asked.

"Darling," she said to me, "the day before Granny died, she confessed something. You have to promise not to tell anyone what I am going to tell you. Anyone!" I said nothing. "Something about Pearl," she whispered.

"What?"

"The night before she died Granny told me something."

Pearl with her fat face, acne that lingered till her sixties. Good at making lemon meringue pies, but stripped of the talents she'd once had. She'd been bright, once and artistic. Poor woman. That sunny disposition buried under the detritus of an over-domesticated marriage.

"Before Pearl met him" (whose lack of finesse in everything was the cause of her misery), "she loved someone else!"

"Who?"

"They disapproved of him. You know. In those days . . . They wanted the best for her. They didn't trust the man."

"What happened?"

It was over, and Pearl was heartbroken but they believed she would recover. They sent her to learn shorthand and typing. Ridiculous, given that she was the first woman in the family to go to university. Anyhow – the man wrote to her, wanting to see her again."

"Go on . . ."

"Granny was in the house on her own when the letter arrived."

This was when Granny's ghost appeared to me for the first time. She, it, stood rigid behind my mother, watching in horror. I witnessed this. I saw her eyes, startled, beseeching, radiant. Ice cold. Life in death. Death in life. The air in the room. Our eyes met. My live ones, her forever dead ones.

"She opened the letter and she read it," my mother went on. "Then she tore it into a hundred pieces. But when she knew she was close to death, she could not face God without telling someone, so she told me. And now you must promise me that you will never tell another soul. No one in the whole world, ever."

§

I grew up, and set about mixing with writers. Real ones, as opposed to ones like me. What real writer vowed never to share the best story that came their way. Tales that brought a tightening to the chest, a turning of the stomach. They were easily identified as the ones not to be told. At moments like this, I glimpsed my beloved Granny. She would flicker there, in front of me, her steely eyes warm with compassion for my predicament. Because it was she, she all along, who had taught me to love stories.

Admittedly, the ones she recited, her back against the net curtains of our dining-room, were in German. Born in a corner of Eastern Europe, she recited for me the authors whose names had lit up her life. Unschooled in Jewish learning, she had schooled herself elsewhere, and found in her heart a passion for romantic epics. Goethe, Schiller, Heine, page after page, verse after verse. Words I didn't understand, yet I understood the way her body leaned into the air as she recited them.

When I was thirty I encountered Melanie Codie. *The*. She and I attended the same writing group and chatted over glasses of wine about the vicissitudes of child-rearing and marriage to unpleasant husbands.

Her career blossomed when she divorced hers, and I envied her. He did her three favours, this badly-behaved spouse. The first was having an affair with an occupational therapist, the second was punching Melanie on the cheek when she refused to make dinner twice in a week. The third and best was this. He moved out, leaving her with a young child and a Norwegian lover who was an avant-garde artist in glass. Her first novel was about a husband who punched his wife; her second was about a woman looking for new love who encountered an artist whose work was cold as steel. With a prize-winning film script she mined what turned out to have been an enviably harsh childhood in another country altogether. She held the infidelity plot in reserve until she published her fourth, impressive and best novel, about an unfaithful husband.

I could not compete. By this time I was married to James – and he was genuinely not unpleasant. I loved him. I'd loved Granny Malin too. I loved my mother also, although for some years my urge to become a writer and hence no respecter of secrets, hung over us like a shadow. We both knew that if I told tales I would lose my sense of morality.

There was one year where things almost improved. James' colleague Katy declared her love for him suddenly, and for months I imagined that he might have the decency to conduct at least one small affair – thereby giving me carte blanche to write about a disintegrating marriage like Melanie Coda's.

But it didn't work. Katy left voluntarily and although she told James she was devastated to be saying goodbye, all that happened was that she rested her head on his shoulder, sniffed snuffily, and left snot stains on his shirt. The shirt went in the wash and that was the end of it.

Last year I paid a visit to my parents. They welcomed me lovingly as always, and sat me down in my old armchair, while we prepared for a catch-up. My mother might have lost the fear of my youthful desire to be a writer, but I knew that our problem was still there. Because the moment I walked in, Granny Malin made herself known to me. She shimmied on and off the curtains, skirted her way round the dining-room table, bent low over my hair, whispering cheekily that I was almost grey myself now. I felt her breath on my face.

"We have sad news," said my mother. The news was Suzi Elterman was terminally ill. They'd moved to London, Suzi and Karl, not long after I left home, but the friendship between them and my parents had lasted. Suzi and my mother still spoke frequently.

There had been a phone call in which Suzi revealed a dark assessment of her health. She was dying. In a few weeks she would require round the clock nursing. Next thing Oliver reappeared back home for the duration.

"The duration of what?" my mother asked Suzi anxiously. "What do you mean?"

"You know what I mean. We talked about it for years."

Oliver had fulfilled his brilliant beginnings. He was a scientist, an architect, and a philosopher. He mixed in high echelons in countless countries. Google registered several thousand references to his works.

"The other day I spoke to Suzi, and Karl came to the phone too. He said they were having a few relaxing days, and he was occupying himself with writing letters. We can expect a letter too, because we are old friends and neighbours. He sounded so calm. It was terrifying."

"What do you think he meant?" I asked.

"He said Oliver will be with them for another week or two and then it will be over."

A plan was made. My parents would go to London to see dear Suzi and to support Karl. I would go with them, and we would aim to visit them this week. So Granny Malin stayed around, to keep an eye on me.

Was this not an irresistible story unfolding? Might I not decide to tell it, one day?

A week later when we set off for London, she sat beside me, on the back seat of the car, as my mother drove, and from the front my parents shared with us, sotto voce, what they feared were the intentions of their oldest friends.

Karl was making sure to enjoy the last fortnight of his life. He was in excellent health, unlike Suzi who was in bad pain. He relished the stimulus of Oliver's company. Oliver was going to help them.

"How?"

Granny Malin was behaving like a character in a pantomime. There she is, she's behind you! Oh no she isn't, oh yes she is! Sometimes a ghost, sometimes a warning, sometimes a figment. In through one car window, out by another. Flitting, skitting, she gave me palpitations.

§

Karl and Suzi lived in Richmond. Initially they'd kept an elegant pied-a-terre which they shared with Oliver. Now they had a flat in a house of huge proportions. Suzi's Bechstein grand looked tiny under the high ceilings of this converted palace.

"Do they know we're coming?" I asked my mother.

"No. But we want to talk to them. Just, you know, pay our respects." Granny Malin glanced at me disapprovingly. She sensed all too well the thrill I was feeling. I was a hound about to be unleashed.

§

We parked. My mother went first, up the six steep steps that led to the front porch. My father and I stayed put in the car. We watched as she bravely knocked on the door. The curtains were half open. Deep, velvet, doubled back curtains. There was a light on in the living room. After knocking three times, my mother came back to the car, climbed in, and said,

"Perhaps they've gone for a walk."

"Not a walk . . ." whispered Granny Malin knowingly in my ear.

"Why not phone them?" I asked. Just then a shadow passed by. No, not a shadow, but a distinguished looking man in a dark suit, and it was Oliver, whom I hadn't seen in years. He had a beard now to match his status and somehow had inherited his parents' mid-European manners. He bowed towards us. This avenue was so posh it defied the laws of nature. On most other streets trees close to buildings were a threat and could ruin foundations. But here giant ash and hawthorn, oak, lined the pavement yet the buildings were unimpaired. The trees sent their roots carefully in the opposite direction to avoid causing damage underground.

"What a surprise," Oliver said stiffly, "I have just come to see my parents."

"I thought you were here already," my father said bluntly.

"I was, just for a while, and now I am back, to see how they're getting on." He took out a key. "Would you like me to give them some message?" His voice was cool and his tone considered.

"We know how ill Suzi is," said my mother to Oliver, "but I had to come and see her. Unless she doesn't want to see me." Oliver moved to the steps, climbed four, turned round. His body language was a puzzle, both to me and to Granny Malin, who looked from him to us and back again.

"I am sure they will be pleased to see you." Oliver seemed to relent, and turned the key. "So come in, do." He pushed open the door, and motioned to my mother, courteously. And I watched as he and she entered the house, Granny Malin slipping in with them. My father stayed in the passenger seat, and I waited in the back.

What happened next happened both at great speed and in slow motion. Some minutes after my mother disappeared into the house I looked up and saw her reappear at the front door, white as a ghost. She looked terrified. She swayed, at the top of the steps, then shuddered and began to descend. She took four steps down, and then seemed to forget there were two more. The two she overlooked were the deepest. She plunged heavily to one side, and crashed down onto the cobbled pathway. I thought she was dead, and I screamed.

§

It was a miracle that she survived such a fall, but survive she did. All the while I sat beside her hospital bed, me on one side, my father on the other, and all the while Granny Malin sat with us. We didn't talk.

My mother was unconscious at the start, then barely conscious for a few days. If a ghost can seem thoughtful, then that was what Granny Malin seemed. On the fifth day my mother began to say things, though it was hard to make out what. She had fractured her jaw in addition to the other injuries and was wired up. I think she said, "I saw them. I saw them both. Owiver koo. Karl was on the floor. Killows. Koo killows. Owiver cook the killows away."

Her last day in hospital, she could speak slightly more clearly, but now it seemed she didn't want to talk to me. Just thank you thank you for staying with us darling. Go home now, go home to James.

§

I had a life, and a sense of something wholesome, with James. We had our children, now grown up, and a holiday cottage in Wales. Granny Malin rarely bothered me at home. She knew me for what I was, and I knew her for what she was – my unfulfilled lifelong search for hidden tales. Either I should not tell them, or no one should tell them, or no one should ever have told them.

Two weeks later I was back home, cooking lamb stew. James and I chatted about the story of my parents' old neighbours, their lives, their deaths. Their lies, or rather their son's lies.

This followed the phone call from my father who suggested we should not talk about the incident again - certainly not bring it up with my mother because she was still suffering excruciating pain from her fall, and would never recover from the shock of what she saw when she entered the lounge with Suzi's Bechstein in it. Two bodies on the floor. The plastic bags. The pillows. Oliver stepping forward carefully, his back to her, bending down and removing the pillows. The way he turned around and stood, looking through her. He carried them through to the kitchen, my mother thought afterwards.

We sipped an aperitif, and read once again the two-page spread in The Times about the peaceful ending of two noted intellectuals, who had agreed to die together. Their son Oliver was inter-viewed at length and spoke respectfully about his parents, saying that above all he was pleased they died together, peacefully, side by side. No suffering.

Side by side? asked the interviewer. Yes, replied Oliver, on their bed. At peace.

James and I marveled at the complex morals of the world outside our home, as opposed to the straightforward ones we lived by. The lamb stew stayed in the oven an hour longer than it needed to and became ultra-tasty. It had in it red wine, carrots, tomatoes, olive oil, garlic. We agreed it was the best stew ever.

Then one evening a flicker of movement behind the TV caught my attention. A shadow. Surely not? Yes, it was. I sensed a presence, and as I sensed it, the phone rang, and it was my father again, sounding weary, because they were not young, and my mother had still not recovered from her terrible fall. The stress of it. But something else. Aged Aunty Pearl was in hospital now, and desperately ill. She was in her late eighties. A widow. Two daughters far away. One in New Zealand, one in Moscow for a year. My mother came on the phone too. "Please darling, do this for me. I simply don't have the strength yet. Go and see Pearl for me."

§

I am actually not a morbid person. After a brief period of adolescent moodiness, I had emerged into the adult world as normal as anyone. My desire to be a writer was a fire that I allowed to burn out. Over the years I had never seen much of Pearl, either. She still lived in Lancashire, where it still rained. But now my mother said I ought to visit her. And Granny Malin, bless her reappeared the minute I stepped onto the train - refreshed, persistent, if nervous.

James called my cell phone as I walked into the hospital, and we agreed with good humour that it was simply a matter of age. The older generation, those who were still alive, were now very old. We ourselves were on the cusp of old age. Granny Malin was way past it.

Pearl was out of intensive care, and in a small white room. On her bed lay a copy of Elle of all things. All the drab decades now behind her, she seemed to be enjoying flicking through the pages. A svelte woman paraded in a taupe skirt and five inch heels. Her lips glistened in opaque peach and glossy fuchsia. When Pearl saw me, she held out thin bruised arms in welcome. Dull husband long dead, daughters noticeably absent - all she had was a visit from a niece who had somewhat neglected her, and of course, her late and loving mother, Granny Malin close by. In fact, my ghostly companion sat wringing her hands at the bedside of her once deceived daughter as if she was auditioning for a role in a remake of an old Yiddish film.

"My favourite niece!" Pearl said, looking warmly pleased to see me. "Come and talk to me, tell me how you are. How is your lovely husband?"

"James is fine thank you. He sends his love."

"Your James," she said, "has always reminded me of someone I once knew. A very long time ago. Before I was married. Would you believe it? In those days I was a bright young thing too – like the women in this magazine!" I smiled appreciatively. "But he wasn't trustworthy like your James. He was a bit of a good for nothing. And I'm not afraid to tell you – he broke my heart. I hope you're not shocked."

"Make her understand," murmured the voice in my ear, "tell her something, something between what you know to be true, and what you know will make her happier. Find a way of telling her she was loved, without telling her that I tore the letter from a man who loved her into a hundred pieces."

"I don't know what to say," were the useless words I came up with.

"I always had a soft spot for your James," she said. "He used to remind me of someone I once knew." Then she said that again. Twice.

§

Do I feel an urge to gather her in my arms, and tell her truthfully that way back when she was young a letter came for her? Yes, but I overcome it. Because I cannot follow the revelation with the other truth. Your own mother betrayed you, even though, or perhaps because, she loved you! Is that it? Was that it? Just get over that minor event before you die.

When Pearl holds out a shaky hand, I see she has Granny Malin's thick wrists, and I remember Granny in my childhood, sorting odd socks, never allowing one to be left alone with no partner. Sweet. I turn for a minute to stare at my imaginary muse, and notice she has become still, for the first time. She's waiting. She'll wait forever, for me to decide what should have happened.

The Emissary

You're waiting in International Departures. You're flying British Airways to Tel Aviv. To your left, a young Israeli woman, a purple scarf turbaned around her forehead. To your right, a black-coated clergyman with a weak mouth sits benignly, a cross on a silver chain around his neck. Yards away a group of youngsters pose for photographs, popping cans of Coca-Cola.

We'd met for lunch, you and I at the art museum. After exchanging pleasantries, we talked about some of the exhibits. We admired a collage of congealed semolina and pistachio nuts. The slits in the nuts were like mouths in tiny faces and made me smile. Over coffee, I told you I was going to Israel to visit my parents but at this particular time was not that keen to go.

"Send me," you said. "Your emissary." You added, "I could do with a week away."

§

The plane cuts heavenward through clouds. From your window seat you look past the smooth wing to grey slices and green patches of England.

You've landed amongst a group of Born Again Welshwomen. They offer you love and mints. Across the aisle is an orthodox Jewish couple. The mother is less than twenty. The baby on her lap gurgles. Her dress hangs down over knee-high boots, and a scarf covers her hair. The husband wears a black suit and black hat, in the style of urban Poland, nineteenth century.

The mother opens her high dress beneath the towel she has draped over her chest and puts her baby to nurse. You smile at the baby`s small protruding feet. A steward approaches the couple and the young man shoots out an arm to warn him off. Nein! he protests in Yiddish.

§

Outside the airport you queue for a taxi. It`s dawn and you`re yawning. Behind you a man with fuzzy hair is reading a paperback. Walter Benjamin. In his travel bag you note Proust and the New York Times. Questions form in your mind about the nature of Jewish culture, Israeli culture, and thoughts rise in opposition. Betraying Christine, you think to yourself. She might never forgive me for doing this. The man examines his fingernails.

In the taxi you remember what he reminds you of. He`s next to you, in the back, hunching his shoulders. That morose self-absorbed look. You saw that, in mirrors, all the time your first wife was leaving you. The one you talked about when we met. We were young then and we all wanted to be writers.

When I enquired why your first wife had left you, you explained that it was straightforward really. She had someone else all along. Someone closer to what she was really like.

"Do you still miss her?" I asked.

"What I miss is not her, but rather - aspects of myself, that I could only express through knowing her."

The self-absorbed man gets out of the taxi before you, disappearing into a block of flats built of chunky Jerusalem stone. You give the driver the address I gave you - my parents' flat. And here you are, in the Israel Mark and I chose to leave, the Israel the world can't handle anymore, the Israel Christine despises passionately. I know this from her Facebook comments - they make me shiver.

You blink in the sharp morning sun.

§

"This will come as a surprise to you," you'll start, and my father stares at you, baffled.

"But come on in," my mother urges, half way through your explanation.

You look round their first floor flat. On one wall, Japanese prints; on another, a Mexican bark rubbing. A brass etching, framed in oak, is of interest to you. A distant relative, who lived in Paris between the wars, made this. He perished in Bergen Belsen.

They invite you, my emissary, to make the flat your base while you're in Jerusalem. There is the room all ready for me, with the faded bath-towel I used as a child. Tough, faded, it's still mine. The bed's ready for me, but you'll sleep in it.

And you're invited to tour Jerusalem. The press Israel gets abroad is bad and getting worse. They want you to see for yourself. They suggest you go and look at the wall – both walls. The ancient western wall, part of the second temple. And the dividing wall, built to keep out suicide bombers. (Both you and Christine call it the apartheid wall.) But you decide to catch the light rail down to the Old City and reach the Shuk. You stop to buy a pair of sheepskin slippers for Christine. The Palestinian shopkeeper is a plump smiling woman, and you tell her it's a present for your wife.

Later my parents question you about us. "How are Mark, Leora and the children?" They expect you to know, being a friend of the family. My father enquires where your family comes from. You say smilingly – just Norfolk.

In a relaxed mood, you watch late-night news on television. News in Hebrew, Israel news, CNN, Sky, followed by Jordan's late-night bulletin in English. The Middle East is now the centre of the world for you. There is a sensation in you of old dreams. Perhaps you had ancestors who were crusaders, and it's their path you're retracing.

My parents have heard about you, of course. Our friends Christine and Harold. Harold an anthropologist and a theatre critic, Christine a maths teacher.

You clean your teeth using toothpaste from a tube with Hebrew letters on it. You think about your children, and your garden with its hydrangeas and roses. You think of Christine's final tearful ultimatum: if you go to Israel, now, it will be the last straw. I dislike that country, and for good reason!

I've no idea what you'll make of Jerusalem itself. The light sky, the exuberant traffic, the smells. The Old City. The western streets. Blocks of apartments surrounded by lantana bushes, oleander, pines. The Mount of Olives. The voices of the Muezzin across terraces and traffic jams. The cool breeze at sunset, and the blues and reds of dawn, where the sky splits and the city is pierced by shafts of light.

Next day you plan to visit my sister, as I normally do. In a farewell walk in Jerusalem you pass olive trees on terraces two thousand years old and enjoy the vista of Jerusalem pines. The trees here are not like English trees. The olive trees have a more silvery hue. Thistles prickle against your shoes, and cats leap about in the sun.

§

My sister Rachel asks herself if you and I are lovers. It is her first thought, as she, her husband Simon, and their five children welcome you to their villa on the Moshav. A tiny village on the edge of the Negev desert, ten minutes from Gaza.

Christine said: how can you have agreed to do this? At such a time?

They offer you olives, yoghourts, green peppers. My brother-in-law brings dust in from the fields where he grows onions and watermelons. With flashbacks to our teenage years that are visceral, Rachel weighs you up. She watches as you bend to stroke the dog, Galileo.

"Explain one more time, will you? You're a friend of Mark and Leora's?"

"Yes. A good friend of both of them," you say firmly.

On Shabbat afternoons, the computers down, air-conditioners on time-clocks, cars all silent, my sister enjoys racy novels set in Bangkok, New York, Afghanistan. Spies, criminals, sexy businessmen, and women engage in illicit, turpid love affairs. You wouldn't guess.

Starting to relax, she offers you a tour of the Moshav. As you walk down the pathway, birdsong harmonizes with your footsteps. She confesses to missing English custard pies and buses. You tell her about Christine's love of orchids, cacti, and crosswords. You don't tell her that the last time I phoned you at home, Christine called out in celtic sing-song,

"Your friend Leora's on the phone, dearest. Again."

By the second evening on the Moshav, you're sitting comfortably on the sofa. Galileo positions himself on your toes, heavy and warm.

The talk gets nearer the bone. We might get rockets tonight. When a warning comes, we have fifteen seconds in which to move into that little room. A mamad, it's called, in Hebrew. Israel only ever bombs Gaza after hundreds of rockets have been fired at us, my sister wants you to know. You already do, actually, because I have told you that. But then you and I have agreed that that is rarely the whole story. Nothing ever is.

Tomorrow, anyway, you are on your way. You're going to Ashkelon, which we left, to see Rafi and Timna, who left each other.

Rachel still hopes you might visit Galilee to meet cousin Ayala's husband, and understand how he gets on with Arabs.

"But you ought to see how they live." Christine's anxious voice in your head won't let you forget Gaza. She's been there, seen it. My sister waves a photograph at you. It's Ayala's son, at an International Mathematics Competition with his friend Mohammed who is Muslim, Palestinian and Israeli. Mohammed wants to be an astronaut, and fly to the moon. Then Christine's voice in your head shouts:

"The West Bank! Gaza! An army of occupation. It is apartheid, whatever they tell you!" Your mission is on my behalf, you remind yourself, whatever the cost. But it's a pain, you feel the mess of it like a real pain.

Next morning you take leave of the Moshav. My brother-in-law gives you a lift to the bus stop at the bottom of the hill, shakes your hand, says goodbye. You wait for the Ashkelon bus, under high eucalyptus trees.

§

At Ashkelon Bus Station you dial the number I have given you. The contrast between the shade of the bus station, and the brilliance of sun striking the street outside hurts your eyes. Rafi picks up.

"Old New Tours . . . can I help you?"

"I'm a friend of Leora and Mark's . . ."

"Then you must come over!" he insists warmly.

He has an office upstairs, the walls painted stucco like the outside of a house. In fact, you're inside an old Arab house, in what was once the village of Majdal.

Rafi and Timna didn't live in Ashkelon, as we did. They had a weekend cottage (later, Timna's home) and Rafi's business, organizing pilgrim trips to the Holy Land. Evangelical Christians mainly. I went to him to ask for help. I said, feeling shaky,

"Will you book us tickets for England. I've got to leave."

"No," he said flatly. "I can't go behind Mark's back like that." Then, more gently, "And you shouldn`t run away from things, either. Face things. It`s better."

"Is that what you and Timna do?"

A few days later Rafi came to our flat. Mark had taken our little ones to the beach to watch the sun set. In minutes it would turn red and misty – then vanish in the sea.

"Do you want a drink?" I asked him. I found him stupidly attractive.

As he gulped a glass of water I began to cry. He had a way of standing. He ran his fingers through his thick hair. When he put out a hand to wipe the wet off my cheek I felt like an illustration in a magazine. Rafi said deliberately, "The best thing is to talk openly."

So I said, against his warm fingertips, "Just that I want to leave Israel. I don`t want to be here." He stepped back, and away. You know, Timna had been flaunting her relationship with a young lover. This had caused him agonies or whatever. I'm telling you all this. You know as well as I do that people aren't machines.

"Ah! So you want to leave Israel, as a way of running away from your feelings?" This was the voice of the encounter group they were attending, run by a Canadian psychologist.

"I don`t want to run away. I would like to go back to England."

I didn`t kiss him. But I wanted to. So I moved away, straight into the bathroom, and locked the door. When I heard the front door close I emerged from the bathroom. Mark and the children came back. They had sand everywhere – between their toes, and in their mouths. I knelt between my sand-encrusted children, thinking of the only other time Rafi had touched me. He was leaving for army service, and came to say goodbye in uniform. I allowed myself to hold him then for a second because Timna was having an affair with a man she met on the beach at night, and I thought Rafi might die.

He cross-examines you. "Where are they at now, Leora and Mark? Has Leora got herself into some sort of therapy? She needed it."

"She goes to meditation classes. Does that count?"

"Come for dinner," he insists. "Any friend of Mark and Leora's. My new wife is making beetroot soup."

§

Tonight Christine is on a chilly all-night vigil outside a Cathedral, in support of Palestinian women. She feels sick and anxious at this journey of yours through Israel. The injustices done to the Palestinians by Jews and Israelis weigh more heavily on her than all the other injustices in the world. But Timna will be curious to meet you, I'm certain. By the time you've been sitting on her low grey cushions for an hour, listening to Sibelius – you`ll feel, I think, that this was probably the real purpose of your journey.

You find her, initially, disturbing. She does not appear to be the kind of person you would immediately find intriguing. But neither do you to her. Her dark complexion is lightened by gold-rimmed spectacles. She takes them off to wipe her eyes, laughing at your description of Mark and me trying to learn bridge.

Describe for her the time we set off, you and Christine, Mark and I, on a country walk last December. Christine asked Mark, "Why do you think it is that Jews don't want to be like the rest of us?"

Mark replied that it might be because "the rest of us" sometimes asked insulting questions. Christine smiled blandly at him, unbothered by his irritation.

It was very windy. We walked on, the four of us, up a sharp peaky hill where hang-gliders con-gregated.

"Go on, please," Timna encourages you. You're evoking the English countryside. She is absorbed by the way you enunciate words. In our years in Ashkelon I was a misfit, inasmuch as I wanted to leave the place. But her problem was worse. She felt a misfit everywhere, and weekends by the sea were not the answer.

§

So Rafi would come on his own. Timna would be off to photography, re-birthing, gestalt, circle-dancing. Sometimes she took the children, some-times she left them with Rafi.

In dazzling sun now you stroll together in the park, under eucalyptus and sycamore trees, past crusader gun emplacements, orange-groves. She and I sat here, while our children climbed over the warm stones of the ruined Byzantine Church. Or peeped under the lid of the Roman sarcophagus which lies perched above the grassy hollow you've now reached, you and she. Look around, will you? Find what it was I wanted, in the many hours I spent here, like a second adolescence, in my twenties?

Our children would scramble over the half-crumbled torso of the Goddess Isis, holding up her son Horus. Timna would talk about her need to escape. But from what and to what? She wrote poems about journeys through tunnels, into light. She's asking you about me, now. You're saying:

"We seem to be able to talk about anything, that's all." Timna watches your face, your Anglo-Saxon features, blue eyes half closed against Israeli sun.

"Are Leora and Mark all right?" she asks searchingly, shading her eyes. "I mean - really."

"They`re absolutely fine."

She peels you an orange, scattering the peel on the grass. The setting evokes in you a hazy excitement, but you look distant and calm. Over there are the ruins of two Arab cottages, swathed in thistles and thick ivy. Through the crumbled doorway, there is a diamond patch of sea. In front of the cottages, an entourage emerges from cars on the gravel path. Out of one car climb a bride and groom. Out of the second comes a wedding photographer in pink jeans, carrying a tripod.

The assistant arranges the couple against ruins and ocean. Their happy smiles in front of the ruined properties evoke in you a sense of curiosity. You sense the conflict, its rights, wrongs and ruins. This ancient place, Ashkelon. Romans, Turks, the British, all tried to possess it. Now it`s a town of pale blocks of flats full of Israelis.

A clutch of raucous ravens swoop down to snatch up Timna's peel. They curve up into the air, orange splashes in their beaks. She says quietly,

"We came here for photographs when we married." You imagine processions of newly-wed couples, parading around this hollow of stone gods. You and Christine, laughingly leaning on each other. Mark and myself, me in a white dress.

§

181

A splendid sunset takes place behind you as you and Timna stroll towards her cottage. Sand scattered on the tarmac makes soft sounds under your shoes. Inside, she makes you up a bed in the room her children slept in before Rafi marched in one day and took them away. She points out the door of the mamad – you need to know where it is.

As darkness falls, notions of why I appointed you as my emissary, why I imagined this journey for you, fill my head. Might it be there are aspects of myself I miss - even though I fought hard for us to be able to leave first Ashkelon, then Israel? Any more of these hypotheses will be as useful to the world as the silvery fish you and Timna will find on the beach tomorrow. Washed up by winter storms, they'll glitter under your feet.

You won't go into her room. She won't come into yours. You lie down on the small bed. Your eyes move across whitish plaster on the walls, cracked in places. Outside, through the wooden shutters, you hear crickets, and the swish, like watery heartbeats, of sprinklers on thirsty lawns. Beyond that you hear the deeper rhythms of the sea.

Verity Thomas

I had wanted to become a therapist, but an illness from which I had recovered – after two whole years – left me doubting everything. My stamina, my mental state, my ambition. From the life of a mental health social worker, a busy wife and mother, a would-be writer - to a world of empty horizons. Some journey. At the time at which I rented a room from Cam Smith, a five minute walk from home, I was vulnerable perhaps.

"I feel OK now," I would insist, because I did, physically. I smiled at myself in mirrors, and hoped to believe in God again – so I would be able to say thank you for the fact that I now felt fine.

Cam had turned his large Edwardian house into a therapeutic hub. Counselling was all I dared to call it. At a pinch - and only with certain people – I would allow myself to call it psychodynamic counselling.

I phoned Amy Brown, whom I'd met at a Psychodrama Christmas Party, because I knew that as well as being a therapist herself, she offered supervision to counsellors of all kinds. Within weeks I had a practice. One day a week (enough to start with) four clients, and a once a monthish supervision with Amy. Did I know her well enough? No. But she'd made an impression. I saw her as intelligently creative. She wore a deep purple pashmina, and to my inexperienced self, emanated something esoteric. At this time I harboured a notion that I would one day train as a real therapist.

§

Of the dozen clients I saw over three years, I only remember Verity Thomas. Not her real name, of course, but that's how I remember her. She bent like a willow as she held out a hand to shake my hand, then jerkily pulled it away.

I had positioned two chairs with wooden arms and highish backs set at an angle to each other. Glancing nervously round the high-ceilinged room, Verity made for the chair by the window, but before sitting down, she nudged it with her foot, so she might be further away from me. She glanced over my shoulder, above then behind me, then turned to examine the corner of the room, where I had placed a bookcase made of rattan straw.

"Hi," I said, although I'd already greeted her at the front door. "I'm Kathy. Do you mind if I ask where you heard about me?"

"The notice board in the library."

"Right. Thanks. Are you comfortable?"

"Yes".

"So. You should know that in a first session with a client, I don't like to say too much. This time this space is for you. I'm more likely to listen."

"Okay."

That was the last thing she said to me at our first session. She sat curled up in her chair, looking at her feet. Once or twice she sighed, and moved her long legs. I began to worry, both for her and for myself. It had not occurred to me that a client might sit for fifty-five minutes and say nothing at all.

"I think you might be feeling a bit anxious. That is all right. This is your time. I'm here."

"Just to remind you? We have another twenty minutes."

"Can I please check whether you would like another meeting? Same time, next week?"

"Yes," she finally spoke, "I would." She slipped out of the room, made for the huge porch and door. As she walked down the path to the gate, she turned and almost smiled, but then didn't.

§

It was impossible for me to speed things up, though I tried. In the third session, I said gently, "Maybe you might tell me a little about why, when you saw my notice in the library, you decided to come and see me?" The suggestion was rewarded with a shrug, then wordlessness until she stood up to leave. But when she came back the following week, she smiled sheepishly and said quite spontaneously, "Hello".

In session five Verity began to talk a little. Much of the meeting was still spent in silence. But I could tell that the quality of the silence was changing. It was becoming a warmer, more relaxed kind of quiet.

After this fifth week, I had my first supervision session with Amy. I drove to the other side of town, parked outside the house which contained her consulting room. The building belonged to a Consultant Psychiatrist, Dr Rosemarine Bookerman. I read the sign in burnished gold. Amy's room was on the first floor. A small room, with chairs set out. As I sat waiting for our supervision session to begin, I had an impulse to play the same game that Verity had been playing. Say nothing. See the effect it had. But of course, I didn't. Instead I did my best to describe my slowly developing relationship with a troubled young woman, as thoughtfully as I could. I believed Amy would help me understand.

§

Verity Thomas was born in Australia, and came to Britain at the age of five with her parents. Something happened. There was an accident or an illness or both. She never gave me full details with clarity, but the outcome was that her birth parents vanished from her life. She was adopted by the Thomas family who lived in Suffolk. There was an older brother, Leonard Thomas. From the outset, she found him bullying and dishonest.

"I have a brother too," I revealed, at my second session with Amy. "My brother Jack is as unlike Verity's brother as he could possibly be."

"Is he?" Amy leaned towards me. On the day that this happened I recall she was swathed in the purple pashmina again. Under it she was in black. She was not much older than me. The material of the pashmina caught sun from the window, and shimmered. She reminded me of a Pre-Raphaelite painting.

"Oh yes," I enthused. "Not that I didn't hate him for a few years when we were young. But I love him to pieces now. And his wife is like a real sister to me. Yes," I added, "I'm lucky there." Amy took notes as I spoke.

"Is Verity depressed?"

"I don't actually know."

"Do you know much about depression?"

"Of course. I was a Psychiatric Social Worker."

"You say she hardly speaks. That can be a sign of something serious." I thought of the English teacher at school who wrote in my report: Kathy tries too hard to be original. Was I trying too hard to be original again? I thought of the gradually shortening silences between myself and Verity. Week by week, shortening.

"Verity is often quiet, but I have a hunch that she is beginning to use our time . . . well."

"In what way?"

"It's hard to say. She still doesn't tell me a great deal. Fragments, bits and pieces. But I sense that between us we are starting to put together a . . . jigsaw."

"My question is: does she feel that, too?"

"I hope so."

"Kathy," she said directly, "you need to confront Verity once and for all. Spell it out. Ask her if she is now or has ever been . . . suicidal."

§

I bore this injunction in mind the next time we met, but didn't raise the subject of suicide because I saw from the moment she came into the room how Verity had changed gear. Within moments she was talking to me, as if our previous silent sessions had done her no harm at all. On the contrary. Her voice was low but her demeanour was warmer. She talked to me, albeit softly, and with a few pauses, as if she had waited weeks to tell me things. She had!

Her brother. Once the family went on a trip to Cornwall. They got stranded on a beach, at sunset. Leonard told her there were waves that came with the sunset, and crashed all over you, and if she wasn`t off the beach that would be the end. She was nine years old, and terrified. Leonard, already thirteen and a half, pushed her over on the sand, then ran off, calling out, drown then you stupid girl because I hate you.

Verity began to sob. How had the silent young woman of a few weeks back morphed into this writhing figure, twisting and turning in her chair? I felt emotional, and seriously protective, but ordered myself sternly not to stand up, move towards her, put a hand on her shoulder. That was against the rules. My rules. Our rules. I allowed myself the thought that perhaps we hadn't been careful enough to spell out our rules to each other, and I almost reached out to comfort her, but didn't.

Instead I remembered my own childhood visits to the seaside, hero-worshipping Jack as he called out the names of little creatures in rock pools. My heart almost broke for the poor girl I was supposed to be supporting, and - I couldn't help it - I felt an urge to weep too. I also felt, in fact knew that I must control myself and not cry. I exerted all the self-control I could muster. I sat upright, eyes wide open so tears might not spill onto my cheeks. I thought, don't let her see you cry, this is her journey not yours. But I gave in. In a brief gesture, I swept tears from my right cheek, which gave a signal to the tear ducts of my left eye. Trying to be casual, I used both hands to push back curtains of salt tears. In the effort of concentrating like this, gulping back the sobs which threatened, I found my nose was blocked, and I had an urge to sneeze. I withstood that urge, breathing fast, in out in out through my noisy nostrils. In the process of making this effort, I missed what she was saying for quite a few moments. Crucial Moments. I realised I had failed to hear something important when she whispered,

"I have never spoken about this before. Not until today." And I hadn't heard. Not to the end.

I felt knocked back in my ambition to train as a therapist and called Amy to request an extra supervision session. Some highly significant event had been relayed to me and I had been too focused on my own emotions to hear the story.

"What has happened?" Amy asked. She looked weary. She was wearing a dark green tunic, and black and white wooden beads. "Is Verity talking about suicide? Is she in danger?"

I described how I had found myself overcome with emotion, and in trying not to cry, sniffed, sniveled and failed to hear the last thing she had told me. I added, "I know what I would like to do, but I would like to discuss it. Basically, I want to tell her what happened; level with her. Then we will move on."

It was six thirty, I recall, and dusk. Amy sat in the half dark and didn't put the light on. From not hearing Verity adequately two days earlier, I was now not quite seeing Amy. And, as I had should have anticipated, there was a silence. Then she astonished me.

"Tell me more," she said, "about your brother."

"But I actually need to talk about Verity. Should I level with her? Or should I leave things, and hope to pick up what I failed to catch? My hunch is – better to be down to earth and truthful. Then we can go on as before. Do you see?"

At which Amy appeared to turn herself into a human statue. A statue draped in dark green and black and white. I found this unexpected, unjustified and annoying. I looked at my watch with anxiety. I had selected a supervisor without knowing enough about her. Why? After what seemed hours, but was probably a few minutes, I persisted:

"Amy, I don't understand what I am supposed to say, or feel. From what I know of supervision, it isn't the same as therapy. (How much did I know about therapy anyway?) I would like to clear this up. I am pretty sure I know what to do now, but I would like your opinion. Please speak to me."

She didn't. She went dumb, deliberately dumb. Amy, who must surely have known exactly what she was doing, sat with her mouth shut until our half hour session (exactly what she had agreed to) was over. And I left – furious, frustrated, none the wiser. I repaid her by saying neither goodbye nor thank you.

"Verity, last week I was moved when you told me of things that happened to you in childhood. You described a time you and your brother were at the beach. I was moved, I even cried a bit. The power of your story. I sniffed and blew my nose, and missed the last part of what you told me. I'm sorry."

"I told my brother his best friend had been abusing me, touching me, and that I hated it. He said not to worry, that was just what big boys did. But if I told anyone, he knew beyond all doubt his friend would kill me. I was nine."

And slowly, week by week, Verity began to piece together the jigsaw that made up her life. Hers, not mine. I began to learn to distinguish between my emotions, and hers, and after that first occasion, I never cried again in front of her.

Cam's Edwardian semi bore a notice outside: Counselling, Osteopathy, Homeopathy. Cam was a short blustery man whose specialism was hugging anyone kind enough to walk through his front porch. Almost always I came to the house before Verity arrived, and when he threw open his arms and gave me the unwanted bear hug, I tolerated it. One week, I was three minutes late, Verity was early. We entered the house at the same time, and Cam was there.

"Kathy!" he came at me like an overgrown puppy. At the best of times, I found his hugs superficial and unnecessary. At this moment, I cringed and pulled away.

"What is the matter?" Cam stepped back, "What is wrong with a hug?"

"We're just on the way in," I said feeling protective towards Verity, and in we went to my "consulting room." As we sat and exchanged thoughts – she didn't seem bothered about the hug she had witnessed - I grasped something. In the months of listening carefully to this vulnerable young woman, I had come to care deeply about her. She had put her trust in me, which in my opinion was a pretty risky thing to do. I felt seriously protective of her vulnerability – and aware of my own.

"Cam insists on hugging people. I hope you weren't upset."

"Not really," - she surprised me by saying this - "but you need to understand what I'm like. I have a wall. That's how I am. There was a wall between me and Cam when he hugged you. A wall between me and you as well, out there."

"And here?"

"There is always a wall. There has to be."

One day, I promised myself, I will read the scores of books by the great therapeutic minds of post-enlightenment Europe. For now, I had read very few, yet I had in front of me a young woman who was increasingly prepared to confide in me.

"A wall," I said.

"Yes. A brick wall."

Soon after this Verity told me of her desire to go back to Australia, even though she now had no family there. She also told me that there was a man in her life. A post-graduate student studying environmental science. He too wanted to see Australia. I felt a twinge of jealousy when I imagined Verity sailing away, boyfriend beside her, and wished keenly that I had a supervisor with whom I might share honestly some of my feelings about our relationship. Clearly I cared deeply for this young woman. One night I dreamt she turned out to be my daughter. I was the mother who gave her up for adoption, and now I wanted her back. In the dream I wept.

§

Three more months went by. I applied to start training in advanced counseling - the real thing - which would lead me to the next stage – having my own therapy. This in turn would qualify me to train as a therapist myself.

I continued as before. Once a week, I would stroll down the road past cherry blossoms, magnolia and oak, and enter Cam's hub, which now sported a notice saying Psychosocial Alignment Therapy – something he'd invented, he told me proudly.

I found Amy's supervision close to useless. I wanted to confront her with the fact but I was afraid she would despise either me or my counselling skills. I wanted her to respect me, even though I didn't respect her.

With Verity, there was no such problem. We seemed to work together. When I mentioned gently that we should perhaps plan how to end our counselling sessions, she told me gravely that she had thought about this, but the time wasn't right. We agreed to discuss the matter every three months from now on.

Then one day she brought me a book to look at, and I took it. A paperback of poems written by her adoptive father's aunt. She did eventually talk about her parents – both sets - and how they failed to give her any sense of security. I took the book with me to a supervision session.

"I had to make a decision," I said frankly to Amy. "Take it or not take it. I took it. There's a poem in it about Verity's birth parents. Now I can't decide whether to open it or not. What do you think?"

As I heard myself speaking, it came to me that I had seriously regressed, at least when it came to supervision. How ridiculous that I should ask per-mission like this from Amy. She was in purple again, and now that genuinely annoyed me. And as I might have predicted, she ignored the book. She stared piercingly at me, as if it wasn't actually there. The weird outcome was - I felt as if I wasn't there.

"I suppose," I said - because I knew it was the right thing to say, "there is an issue of boundaries here. I shouldn't have taken it. But could we please talk about it?"

§

Carefully, Verity and I discussed and prepared how to say goodbye. Each week, at her request, I reminded her how many weeks we had left. My sessions with Amy were the only cloud that hung over us.

Towards the end Verity vented, finally, some of her anger against her adoptive parents. In a bravura outburst she spoke about her adoptive father, and his unconditional support for Leonard in his career as a hedge fund manager in Canary Wharf with a hobby of hang-gliding.

Although I disliked every supervision session, I blamed my negativity on a lack of reading, training, knowledge, awareness. I resolved to look into whatever issues my parents had passed down to me. It only occurred to me that there was a way out of my predicament when I found myself engulfed in a particularly annoying hug from Cam. Pulling away, I found myself saying, "Cam! I go for supervision to someone who isn`t much help! But I've seen a notice up here. You offer it too, don't you?"

"Delighted to take you on," he said.

§

So now there I was, clutching a small bunch of roses, at Amy's front door, intending to say goodbye as politely as I could. I rang the bell, because the door wasn`t open, which was unusual. The roses were supposed to demonstrate my gratitude.

"I'm Dr Bookerman," said the slight woman who opened the door. "Rosemarine Bookerman."

"I'm here to see Amy."

She half retreated back into the house, then stepped forward again.

"Ah. So. I am really sorry that I have to tell you this, but Amy died two days ago. At least we think it was then. I went upstairs and found her yesterday."

"Oh my God, I don't know what to say."

"Neither do I, I'm afraid."

"Was she ill?"

"Not as far as I knew. There will be a post-mortem. There`ll have to be."

"I brought these," I said foolishly, "I was going to thank her for her supervision and say goodbye."

"You had ended?"

"I was going to. Today. Sorry. It's just . . . someone who lives near me offered. It's a drive to get here, you see. Across town, every time. You know. I am really sorry. Shocked, and sorry." I felt shaky. "Was she ill?"

"Not as far as I knew. No."

The question of how and why Amy died had sent my thoughts and feelings into orbit. I felt faint. And guilty. I felt as if my resentment and incomprehension might have killed her. Or rather – she had killed herself – possibly because of me. The warnings about suicide. She'd been trying to tell me something.

"You look green," said the doctor. "Come inside, and I`ll get you some water. Or sweet tea."

So I went inside, and sat down in the small front room. I wondered why the sofa was shaking lightly, then realised that it wasn't – but I was. Not exactly from grief about Amy. But I was stunned by my lack of understanding of things. People were so complicated.

"Did you know Amy well?" My voice sounded far away.

"No. She rented the flat upstairs. But I liked her. She had a wonderful sense of humour."

Amy with a sense of humour was something I found hard to believe. I was losing all sense of being grounded now. Lost moorings, I thought.

"You're not a therapist yourself?" I found myself asking hopefully.

"Absolutely not," said this woman resolutely. "I am a simple psychiatrist. Never trained in analysis. Not even basic counselling skills.

"Did she . . . kill herself?"

I honestly can't say. There will be the post mortem.

§

I said goodbye to Verity some weeks after this. At our farewell session, she handed me a parcel with a ribbon.

"Careful," she smiled, "it`s heavy."

I opened it. It was a brick.

"From my wall," she said as I stared at it. She had painted it a delicate blue. "I have started to dismantle it. One brick at a time. This is the first one I removed. I wanted it to look bright – and feel real."

We shook hands warmly and I wished her well. We said goodbye. The brick was real. It still is. I keep it in the rockery in my front garden, next to the smoke bush.

About the Books

For Dame Louise Ellman, Labour MP, Liverpool – Riverside. 1997-2019.

They were sitting in the Estate Agent's office, about to sign a contract for a flat on the second floor of a block beside a tube station.

"Sorry," Mary said tearfully, "but I need to be in a house, even if it's a small one." Fred shifted slightly, breathing slowly, conveying the message that he was getting fed up with their moving process. They had decided, surely? London it was. Here they were. The agent lightened the mood.

"Something," she raised an eyebrow elegantly, "just on the market. A flat in a converted house. It has a small garden and might be what you're looking for." She showed them the flat that afternoon. Next day they signed on it.

§

Six months later, Mary is in the garden, talking to her new neighbour. Nothing that she feared has come to pass. Shame on those people in the north who warned them against making the move. This friend couldn't be a better listener, and in return Mary listens to her. They're close to seventy, but they exchange biographies like first year students! She's called Carol. She has two daughters. One lives in New Zealand, and is a midwife. The other runs a pet food store on the outskirts of Los Angeles. People spoil their animals in California. Carol is away a lot, and doesn't always reveal to Mary where she is going. But when she does tell her – it confirms for Mary how lucky she and Fred have been to end up living at close quarters to someone with a stimulating cultural existence.

§

Thirty-seven B, Penwood Lane. Their two bedroom flat is the small half of the downstairs of 37 Penwood Lane, a large double-fronted Edwardian house. Carol's home is the big half of the ground floor plus all the rest – the rest comprising a first floor, and a loft conversion.

At the back of the house, the long garden has been divided into two. Their section is narrow, accessed through the kitchen door. Carol descends into her part of the garden via a majestic spiral stairway which leads from her large veranda. She says it's three times the size she needs. Fred has offered to be her gardener, but so far she hasn't picked up on that suggestion.

On the day of their move, Carol invites the newcomers into her main living room, on the ground floor, where they sit for half an hour in awe. Three of its walls are bookshelves. Hardbacks, paperbacks, books in French, Russian and what Mary thinks is either Hebrew or Greek. After they exit the narrow hall and re-enter their minuscule flat, Mary says to Fred: we are lucky; we have negotiated down-sizing from Liverpool to London, and have landed in a virtual house-share with an interesting and intelligent woman!

§

First Thursday of the month Carol goes out. A shabby car looking like a throwback to the nineteen seventies parks outside and a man in it waits for her. He arrives before seven – or sometimes on the dot of it. Once, Mary happened to be going out herself, to post a letter. She heard that the man was listening to The Archers. That made her smile, as she felt sure that Carol herself was above radio soaps like that. The theme tune wafted on the air behind her.

On the first Thursday of the following month Mary found it hard to get to sleep. It was a humid summer night. She tossed and turned until Fred nudged her and said get a glass of water.

So she let herself out through the front door, just to breathe the night air and glimpse the moon, which beamed gently in the sky. Then she glanced sideways, and saw the musky yellow car, the man in it, and in the passenger seat, there was Carol. It was half past two in the morning and they were side by side, heads moving in a way that told Mary they were deep in conversation.

"But I don't think they're lovers," Mary said to her husband next day, and he just said, "None of our business what they are, is it?"

"I'm just saying. The way they were talking. I could see, it's a platonic relationship." She did not add, but did think, of a superior kind, whatever that meant.

There was a wooden gate in the fence between the large and small gardens. It was lockable from Carol's side, as if to protect from invaders. What kind of neighbours does she think we are, Mary often said jokingly to Fred, we don't need to come and sit in her space, we can enjoy her trees from our own garden!

But one afternoon Carol ostentatiously turned the key, which made a loud click.

"Come and have a drink with me?"

So Mary walked through the open gate and onto Carol's spacious lawn, and they got on to the subject of museums.

"In Liverpool," Mary said, "we had the museum of the history of slavery, and the maritime museum. Then there was the Beatles complex!" She felt a wave of nostalgia for her home town, their down to earth neighbours, and Sefton Park. But she rallied when Carol said, "I'm a member of the Freud Museum."

"The Freud Museum? How interesting."

Mary knew that Freud was a great mind of the twentieth century, and told Carol this. Carol responded with a resume of her role, of whatever it was she did at the Freud museum. Not that the detail mattered.

But in Mary's heart, something began to stir, then, to race, to spin, that took her by surprise. Something about what her new friend was involved in moved her deeply. It unsettled her. A question tried to put itself into words, a query that had a life of its own, somehow. "Have I lived all these years without ever reflecting, seriously, on who I really am? Surely I must be aware that I, like everyone else, have an inner self, an unconscious self. Come on then Mary, it's not too late. Look inward! Find yourself! Not too late."

§

Fred and Mary visited the museum three times. Mary picked up books and pamphlets, while Fred did three surveys of the garden. Then Mary enrolled on a course, "Freud and Contemporary Cinema," but found the lectures incomprehensible. She resolved not to share this fact with anyone – even Fred. I've only stopped going, she told him after two sessions, because the chairs were uncomfortable and one attendee wouldn't stop coughing.

Carol held a host of trusteeships, or director-ships, but never mentioned the names of the insti-tutions concerned. She also knew a number of therapists and psychoanalysts, whose books and articles she would drop tantalisingly into their chats.

Then, finally, Mary learned the truth about the man in the yellow car.

"Thursday evenings?" Carol said mildly, "I belong to a Literary Group."

"Wow. That's the kind of thing I'm getting interested in."

"Then I'll introduce you to Max. Or have you met?"

"I don't think so. Who he?" Mary said in a deliberately childish voice, imitating the affected tone of her least-liked cousin Brenda. She hadn't seen Squeaky Bren for twenty years.

"He gives me a lift to the group. A lifelong friend."

§

One morning Carol phoned to invite Mary for a coffee, and when Mary arrived – Max was there!

"Max, this is Mary."

"I've heard a lot about you," Mary said. Not true, but she said things like that when she was nervous. Max was a tall, slightly lopsided man, or seemed so when he stood up. Solid but not fat, brown eyes and dark receding hair. A little younger than the two women.

"Carol said you're from Liverpool," he offered engagingly. "I have roots there. Once a Scouser, always a Scouser, eh?" He smiled. "My great grandparents left Riga by boat, aiming to get to the new world – and all that. But they ended up in Liverpool. They came to London in the nineteen twenties."

"Reeger?"

"In Latvia. They were Jewish."

The last thing Mary expected was that this intellectual owner of that shabby car might be Jewish. Or perhaps only his grandparents were, or maybe just one grandparent was. But then all those documentaries, and articles, about the Holocaust and Nazis came back to her and she recalled that under Hitler it was enough for you to have one Jewish grandparent and you were doomed. Mary smiled warmly but felt uneasy.

The truth was that when people mentioned Jews, she felt a slight tension. She had no idea why this should be. Maybe it went back years. When she was seven she asked Granny Eileen what a Jew was, because they had one in school. Granny said "They killed Jesus. They tried to kill God but obviously they couldn't, but they got Jesus, because he was half a man."

Brenda, nicknamed by Fred Squeaky Bren, was indeed Mary's least-liked cousin, and she, both Fred and Mary had long suspected, was a bit antisemitic. One day, this cousin came over and affirmed in a high-pitched trill that she detested everything Jews were doing to the world, particularly in Liverpool. Her own MP was an example of how maliciously they tried to control things. Bren wore boots with high heels, winter and summer, and called breasts tits.

"I was on a bus," she said once, "with this huge bag of shopping, and it burst, all over the floor, so this fat guy bent down to help me pick stuff up, but all of a sudden he grabbed my tits, and I yelled at him to piss off, which he did, but all the same. Fucking creep."

"What do you mean?" Mary had asked, when Bren showed her an article on google which demonstrated her point. MP Louise Ellman was definitely funded, she read out loud, by international bankers, all Jewish, and by Israel – a disgusting rogue state. Worst of all, Ellman had openly declared herself a Zionist. A person like that would bring Liverpool to its knees.

When Fred and Mary left the north they invited a few people over for drinks but by then Brenda had moved to live in Morecambe so they didn't feel obliged. But when Mary phoned to say goodbye, Brenda squeaked, "Why North London?"

"The kids. You know why."

"There's a lot of Jews in North London."

Fred said she meant it as a joke.

§

Mary realised that both Max and Carol were looking at her.

"So. Might you consider joining the group?" Max asked Mary seductively.

"We haven't discussed it yet, Max," Carol corrected him quietly.

"But seeing as you asked," Mary jumped in at the deep end, "I would love to join. How does one do it?"

Carol explained. "The group was set up ten years ago, and . . . er, it meets once a month."

"Do you take in new people, though?" Mary felt bold and entitled. Look what moving to London was doing for her.

"Yes, but it's a process. It starts with a person being invited to a meeting. As a guest."

"I hereby confirm that one can bring in a visitor from time to time," Max assured her. He liked her. He wanted her in the group.

§

Three months went by. Mary continued what was becoming her London life, which was not really any different to Liverpool life. Just that there was more of it. Sometimes she took the tube into central London, and entertained herself trying out shops and galleries. She was impressed by the array of stalls in the spectacular British Museum, and spent a morning there acquiring paperbacks, ornaments and a pink bracelet. When Fred asked: "What did you see?" she answered vaguely, "Lots of things!"

At the back of her mind was the thought – I have already been invited to join a literary group. Therefore - no need to tire myself out walking round museums just to prove that I am interesting. And into her mind now, this group floated, like a mirage in a desert, or a vision of something in a mist. And feelings surfaced in her that she hadn't owned before. These were special people, no question. And yes she wanted to be one of them. And then for some reason she remembered Brenda always being crude about Jews, who were also supposed to be special.

"Who the fuck do they think they are?" Bren would squeal. Odd that this should come to mind again. It wasn't as if it was a Jewish literary group. Or at least, no one had said it was.

§

The meeting was held in the home of someone called Ronald O'Hara. Mary went with Carol in Max's car. There were eleven people there, and the book they discussed, which she had forgotten to read, or even order, was called Field of Cows. It was written by a Brazilian author she had never heard of. Out of eleven people, three hadn't read Field of Cows. One disliked anything in translation, one woman's father was dying. One person started it but couldn't get past chapter one. So not having read the book can't have been the reason why, after the meeting at Ronald O'Hara's house, Mary heard nothing from anyone for six months. Carol stopped mentioning the group, and Max neither called nor emailed.

§

Carol continued to be friendly, although it seemed to Mary that she was warmer towards Fred than towards her. This annoyed her, because Fred never showed interest in books. Carol's relationship with him was about gardening. How on earth could two people, Mary wondered, keep going as they did, exchanging anecdotes and bits of information about this flower or that, this shrub or the other.

One spring afternoon Mary came out of the kitchen to see Fred leaning against the partition fence, laughing loudly. Above him, perched on a ladder on the other side of the fence, Carol held aloft an ochre coloured flowerpot.

"I'll hand it to you! Here!" Carol held the flowerpot in one hand and with the other tugged at the floppy plant. Fred took hold of the plant, and the soil disintegrated. It fell like dark snow around him, scattered at his feet.

"Mud. Soil. Plants. All he cares about," Mary muttered to herself. "All he sees in our cultivated neighbour is her garden."

The one single disappointment that Mary and Fred were able to share, was in their son and daughter, on whose account they had uprooted themselves in the first place. The son lived with an heiress from New York in a fully electronic luxury flat overlooking the Thames. No interest in either books or gardens. The daughter lived with husband and children in Tufnell Park and only liked whodunnits - particularly Agatha Christie and Sophie Hannah. The only intimate and humorous moments in Mary and Fred's lives nowadays were when they agreed, at least on this one issue. Moving to London may turn out to have been A Mistake!

But then, for Mary, a tide started to turn. An oasis of hope appeared in a desert of cultural isolation.

Max called, to invite her to another Literary Group meeting. "Come with Carol," he said, "It'll be in my place. I live in Golders Green. The book is Austerlitz, by George Sebald."

So she bought Austerlitz, but couldn't begin to get into it. Nevertheless, on the Thursday, Carol phoned to say she was in the car waiting - so out went Mary, carrying it. They reached Max's home and were welcomed. A compact house, surrounded by rhododendron bushes and hawthorn trees.

"Glad to see you," said Max, to both of them, and she noticed how Carol smiled at him but didn't go near him. This fine platonic relationship, she thought, between two highly educated people. I ought to belong with people like these.

"In here," Max pointed, and they went through a doorway. On the right doorpost, three quarters of the way up was an object stuck on at an angle, with Hebrew on it, or was it Greek. In the room the group of eight gathered. The lighting was poor, but there was enough to read by – just, and to light up the photographs on the wall. One picture stood out. Three little boys, aged six, seven, eight, in blue shirts.

"School photo," Max pointed proudly. "My grandsons." On each little head, hair cropped short above smiling faces, she saw skullcaps like the ones orthodox Jews wore in Liverpool.

"Those little caps?" she asked, suddenly queasy.

"Yes," Max smiled. "They go to a Jewish school." Mary was acutely aware that part of her inner self felt repelled. A squirming sensation which she knew was simply not allowed. Yet she couldn't help it. She was not proud of the feeling, and gave herself a stern telling off. If I decide not to go any further, she said to herself, with this esoteric group, let it not be for that reason, then.

One by one she peered at members of the group to see whether they all looked Jewish, or only some of them did. Ron O`Hara and Dympna were there, and she noticed that Dympna was wearing a silver crucifix, ornate but at the same time plain. Surely, she thought, the group wouldn't allow people in who were clearly Catholics, not if the majority were Jews? Or perhaps in London it genuinely didn't matter anymore. She was aware that if anyone read her thoughts at this moment they might be disgusted. She imagined that if the whole room had to vote for or against her, they would vote against, and throw her out. She had heard about the viciousness of cousin Brenda's so-called Labour Party cronies. She heard Brenda's sad tone in the last conversation they'd had about Jew issues. "There`s a witch hunt going on now." For once, Brenda lowered her voice almost to a whisper. "One person says one negative thing about Jews or Israel – and they`re thrown out. A fucking witch hunt."

Fighting for her survival in what now felt like a demonstrably hostile room, Mary planned an escape strategy. Clearly she would have to leave the group. It was dangerous because eventually someone would catch her saying something and would misinterpret it. They sat there, all of them, in their holier than thou circle, gazes falling gravely upon her one at a time. She felt crushed and small now. The discussion about the book barely touched her. That's how it was, until eventually the evening ended and Carol drove her towards home, as if nothing at all was wrong.

"I enjoyed the evening," Carol chirped, "Did you?"

"Well, I did," said Mary very slowly, "but I have been thinking, actually. Probably this isn't really a group for me."

"Why do you think that is?" Carol asked.

"I'm not up to the kind of stuff you seem to choose. Not really. I have to be honest. Truth is, I'm happiest losing myself in a Regency Romance. Honestly. That's all it is."

"Well," Carol said, after they'd been through two sets of traffic lights, "so long as nothing else made you feel uncomfortable. They're mostly a friendly lot."

"Oh I know. Nice people. No no, it's honestly just about the books." The car hummed its way gently home, through the suburban night.

A Lullaby at Midnight

It's midnight. You've had your eleven o'clock feed. A whole bottle. With sugar. Now they said at the clinic no sugar, but I want you sweetened for the night. I want you to have peace, and give us peace. I put you a heaped teaspoon in.

And I have burped you and changed your nappy. And yet now you lie there screaming your little head off as though I had committed crimes against humanity and you are bloody humanity. What is the matter?

You've got a lovely room. The days we spent papering it, him and me. Look – elephants and beach balls. Pink spring flowers. Little Bo-Peep. They said at the clinic that pretty wallpaper is good for you.

Well look at it. Don't just lie there screaming at me. And what about your toys? I put a teddy in your cot and you threw it out. They said you aren't supposed to be throwing things yet. I said well you do throw things - at me usually.

Your cot sheets are clean. I've changed them twice. I've changed your nappy again. It was a tiny bit wet. So what. Anyone could get to sleep as wet as that. You're not at all sore. I've smeared creams all over your little pink bottom. I've cut your finger-nails with baby scissors so you can't scratch your little face. I've washed gently inside your tiny ears with cotton-wool, and they are as clean as seashells in the land of the fairies. Your nose isn't stuffy. Your bowels are all right. You're nearly six months old, and past the age of baby colic, and anyway you never had baby colic.

You're not ill. Three doctors have seen you this week. Two of them were here today. The pee they took away in a polythene bag last week was normal. There is nothing the matter with you.

And it's not love, either. There's no lack of love in your life. We love each other very much, your daddy and I. Sometimes I think too much. It can't be right loving people like that. I miss him when he goes to work. He misses me when I go shopping. We love each other. And we make love, and it's lovely. That's how we made you. And we love you. And I have been holding you and cuddling you for most of every day since you were born. And talking to you, kissing you, giving you security. That is what it's all about, security. Don't pretend you haven't got it. You've got more of it than I ever had, that's for certain.

It can't be teething. I know that because all our family have been retarded in tooth development. I didn't get my first tooth until ten months. Nor did my mother. Nor did my brothers. But I have still rubbed your pink gums with teething jelly, in case by a trick of genetic fate you happen to be different. I have rubbed until the numbing effect of the teething jelly has lost me all feeling in one finger. So I know you can't be feeling pain in your gums.

Well, what then. What is the matter? Where do you feel pain? What are you screaming about? I don't mind being honest with you, baby, and telling you it's beginning to get on my nerves. And daddy's. Thank goodness he's asleep at the moment. He can't manage without his sleep. He works hard.

Well I work hard too, don't I? What is the cause of your crying? Where is your pain?

I hope I'll have enough patience. Look, I'll tell you something. You've got far far less to cry about than I had when I was little. It's true. I would have told you about that, eventually. When you're older, and you don't scream all the time, I'll tell you things. I was born into a very difficult set-up. I'm glad I don't remember most of it. They split up when I was a baby. I was with an aunt for a few years, who didn't like me very much. Then I was in care, where they did care. But by then I didn't - you know. I remember a huge Mrs Cabbot who kissed me and had a funny smell round her neck.

At sixteen I was sent back home to my mother, but she wasn't happy, and neither was I. I wasn't happy at all in fact until I left home properly and got married.

Then I said to myself, now I'll build the sort of life I never had. When you were born we thought it would make my mum happy at last – coming to visit us, and seeing how well we're bringing you up. But I can't have her visiting here if all you do is yowl your head off.

Damn you, my own flesh and blood, go to sleep. Where does your sorrow come from? What can I do about it? What can I do about anything? Look – everything's all right. Don't worry about the world. You've been born into as pleasant a country as any baby could be born into. It's still a democracy – just. Be thankful we are not refugees. You're you. Nothing to cry about. Nothing. Go to sleep. I need rest. Leave me alone. I can't stand your sobbing anymore. Who are you crying about? Who are you, to cry your heart out like that?

Look, I've cried enough for three generations. I can't take it. I've cried and cried and finished. I'm a grown up now and building myself a simple and a happy life. I deserve happiness. I've been through enough to deserve it. I want happiness for you. If I deserve it, you deserve it too. My parents. The way things were, or could have been. You couldn't know about any of that yet. You're a baby and too young to know. And by the time you're old enough to know you probably won't be interested.

Look. I'll burp you again. Kiss you again. Rock you again. Love you forever. If you'll just stop crying. Look at your streaming eyes. Why are babies' eyes like that? I cry for five minutes and mine are puffy and swollen. I used to hide in the lavatory for hours until my eyes became normal. Yours stay crystal clear and the tears pour out of them like waterfalls in spring. Fresh and clear. Are those real tears, baby, or are you trying to do something to me?

That heart-rending screaming, that monotonous moaning, that gulping hiccupping monstrous weeping. I can't be held responsible for this. You'll tear me apart. You'll tear me and him apart. Where has all this misery come from? It's erupting like a volcano. Misery, sadness, despair. All there in your wailing. You've come back, then, all my misery. Reborn. Revved up, refreshed, ready to start all over again. Is this what they mean by reincarnation? The things I'd spent years trying to cure? I had talked myself out of it all. But now you lie there crying and sobbing as though life had never been worse.

Oh my baby, my darling beloved baby! You're sucking my soul dry, can't you feel? Can't you see that you must settle down and then we will all have peace? Go to sleep. I love you. Shouldn't that be enough?

Talia

1983. The moshav was not far from the sea. North of Tel Aviv, south of Haifa. It was called Yad David, named after a hero of the War of Independence, and the name had been shortened to Yadda. A narrow road led from the little village through orange groves, fields, down to an almost main road. When we first moved to Yadda the narrow road wasn't properly paved. By the time we left, after eight years – when the twins were six - the narrow road was paved but the almost main road was still unreliable.

Forty years on, the main road is a dual carriageway, black tar glimmering in Mediterranean sun. Talia lives in a studio flat overlooking the sea near Haifa, and we live in England. She is no longer married - hasn't been for years. I still am and my husband is still Alan.

§

In nineteen eighty-three I was twenty-five and pregnant with twins. Talia and I had parallel pregnancies with no morning sickness. We strolled through the orange groves of Yadda, full-bellied and full of optimism. Alan was from Manchester and I was from London. Yad David and surrounding settlements were in need of a dentist and he was one.

Talia's husband Eli was not exactly the moshav type, or so Alan and I thought. He was a teacher. He taught in two schools – one in Tel Aviv and one in Haifa, so Yadda was nicely placed between the two. I had a degree in three languages.

"How many?" Talia asked, the day we met at a neighbour's barbecue. Talia was pregnant like me, but I thought prettier looking. Alan got into conversation with Eli, whose English was good, but not as good as Talia's. Alan told Eli that if he was unfortunate enough to get toothache, he, Alan would help out.

"French Spanish and German," I said modestly. "But all three languages are under threat now! Learning Hebrew pushes them onto a back burner." Talia's English was better than good. She didn't flinch at a phrase like "back burner."

"All I ever studied," she said – suddenly I was jealous - "was English literature."

A few months later Talia had Noah, a beautiful baby born with long eyelashes. Weeks later I had the twins. Tom and Ben. We loved our little sons, and strolled through orange groves with them, and drove them to the seaside where they paddled, and ate sand. When they could hop skip and jump, we helped them collect pine-cones from the dry ground at the edge of the moshav. We focused and drifted simultaneously, as mothers of young children do, and were in and out of each other's houses. Or outside on the benches that were placed at strategic points on the paths, under giant parasols. We appreciated the charmed surroundings. Eucalyptus trees and bougainvillea. Pathways between the houses with no traffic, so safe for any toddler. Birdsong every day of the year.

When Noah had a tantrum, Talia scooped him up, cajoling him with promises.

"Come," she would say in Hebrew, "Think what I'll give you if you stop crying! First of all . . . a little dish of ice cream! Then, who knows, Abba will tell you a special story."

"Then something else nice . . ." the little boy would bargain, not remotely consoled.

"Anything you want, sweetie," she would coo. "Tell Ima what you want and you will have it!"

But when the twins got overtired and screamed blue murder, Alan and I practised the English way of discipline.

"We won't listen until you please stop screaming. Then if you ask nicely, we'll see. And no, we don't have ice cream at bedtime."

Talia installed Noah in the Avivi Nursery for Gifted Toddlers, Alan and I enrolled our toddlers in a kindergarten nearby. As soon as we got the taste of freedom a few hours a day, Talia and I began to talk about how to broaden our horizons. When Eli heard us chatting, asking ourselves where we would go from here – here being the daily routines of Yadda – he warned, "Stop feeding each other's demons." One of his American grandmother's idioms.

"Don't worry," I reassured him. I liked Eli – down to earth, a teacher like Talia, and a serious bread-winner. He liked both his schools, and did well. Not an intellectual like his wife. A big mop of unruly hair. Attractive, I thought. "We're not heading for an existential crisis!"

"I wouldn't know one of those," he replied bluntly, "if it hit me in the face!" We laughed. But where was the harm in our looking outward, Talia and I hoping for fulfilment beyond the small spaces of Yadda with its perfumed groves?

Naively, I thought Talia was already half way there. She was deep into a Masters in English Literature at Tel Aviv University. An odd literary journey for a woman born in Israel of parents from Hungary and Czechoslovakia. She carried a note-book which she would flick through, challenging my self-esteem with concepts like structuralism, post-structuralism and other isms. With each page turned, each esoteric concept, I gazed more earnestly at the notebook, which was the colour of red grapes.

Our chats sometimes turned to the topic of her supervisor, whose name was Professor Angelina Conway-Brown. "I am the luckiest student ever," Talia would enthuse, unbothered by domestic disorder of the kind that Alan and I would never tolerate. Piles of washing. Her casual way of sorting it. She threw it on the floor, then warned Eli not to walk on it.

I had heard of Conway-Brown, and read an introduction to one of her books. Literary criticism, or was it meta-criticism? One day I asked curiously if outsiders might attend her renowned lectures, and a week later there we were – Talia had arranged it! Alongside my friend's restless ability to create change and make things happen, I felt static and dull. She drove us both to Tel Aviv on a hot and humid day. The windows had to be open. The traffic and the burning wind, the noise and pressure.

"It's like being in a fan oven!" I complained.

Next I sat at a formica-topped table in the air-conditioned basement of the university, and was introduced.

"This is my English friend Anna. Anna, meet Professor Angelina Conway-Brown. She is super-vising my Master's and I am the luckiest student ever!" Talia fiddled with her fork, shifting tiny cubes of tomato cucumber and pepper from one side of her plate to the other.

"Do call me Angelina. Do you live in Yad David also?" the Professor asked me. She wore glasses with tortoiseshell rims. Her hair was pulled back tightly. Greyish brown. Lines on the forehead gave away that she must be two decades older.

"Yes. My husband and I came here from Man-chester. He's a dentist."

Wrong thing to say. Intellectuals - she visibly was one - do get toothache, of course. But for them a dentist is someone you go to, not something one of your children becomes.

As though she knew I was admiring her as a doyenne of academia, Angelina said, "People know me as an English academic, but if I go back two generations – believe it or not I actually have some family roots here. When I retire I will write a popular novel about the original Angelina. Her real name was Miriam." Talia stopped crunching salad, mouth half open.

"It turns out my paternal grandmother Miriam was a Jewish girl born in Jaffa. She was orphaned at seven, and sent to a Church school there for shelter and an education. She was well taught and cared for. But when she was sixteen – this was nineteen thirty-one – and a Jewish uncle from London came over here to reclaim her, she announced that she'd become a Christian!"

Israeli social history. I knew so little about it. I listened. Miriam Noemi Cohen refused to give up her Christianity, but was forced to marry a Jew anyway – a British one who happened to be visiting Palestine. With her new husband, Mrs Miriam Noemi Brown set sail for the UK, experiencing seasickness and panic attacks during a nightmare honeymoon. Weeks after reaching England, she fled from the husband to take shelter in a Mission House in Norwich, claiming she had been forced to marry in Jaffa. From then on she lived in England as a Christian. Talia gaped, eyes wide.

"How do you know this?"

"Ten years ago," said the slender Professor, "a relative of mine died in Norwich. I went through her papers, and found newspaper cuttings. I was astonished, as you can imagine."

"And you thought yourself quintessentially English," I said intensely.

"Yes, I suppose I did. What about you?" she asked me as if I mattered.

At that moment, something slipped inside me. I felt the touch of new awareness, inner momentum. I climbed a mystical mountain track, up and over a peak to a new and beautiful place, and I stumbled upon truth. I ought to be more like Talia. I was the one who ought to be steeped in the sophisticated teachings of the best British universities. I had wasted my intellect on three alternative languages, while English, the precious gift spoken to me from birth by loving parents, was being stolen from me before my eyes. Talia thought she owned it, but truth was – it should be mine.

"Didn't you like her?" she asked, as we got into the rusted car, which neither she nor Eli ever had time to clean.

The discussions, the plans hatched, the efforts I had made to convince Alan that Israel would be the place for us to grow as a Jewish family . . . After all that, it hit me. I did not belong here. But how could I discuss this with Talia before even starting a conversation with Alan?

We hardly spoke on the way home. Eventually we left the main road and turned up the narrow lane towards Yadda. Home, our little house with its garden, my children being bathed by their loving Daddy.

"I saw how brilliant she is. Thank you for the introduction." Talia was impulsive in ways I later came to view as deranged. But at the time I saw her impulsiveness as a gift.

"Not to worry," she said in Hebrew. Then in English, "I want Eli to meet her also. She keeps asking me about life on a moshav. I'm going to invite her."

§

For the next few weeks we resumed daily chats in our effortless mix of languages. I forgot my Damascene moment in which I admitted to myself that perhaps coming to Israel was a mistake. Talia and I continued to cover most topics - politics, the sea, sex, marriage and of course childhoods. Talia was passionately political. Every Friday afternoon she went to demonstrate against the Israeli occupation of the West Bank and Gaza, and against the settlements which were springing up - no government intervening to stop them - in those areas.

"You don't care about politics enough," she commented critically and I was offended.

"I do. But we made a big move, coming here. It's a small country with a big history. Too much going on. I need to take things one day at a time."

"We must challenge the powers that be," Talia argued, "to change their ideas. Come demonstrate with me." It wasn't that I didn't care about the politics. A few people in Yadda viewed the enthusiasts of the growing Settler movement as unacceptably right wing. But on Fridays Alan went cycling with a group of Yadda friends, while I got the twins ready for the weekend.

§

A month later Talia and Eli invited us to their home a hundred metres away for drinks with Angelina Conway-Brown. Tom wore blue dungarees, Ben wore brown, and they both had new red tee shirts. They looked cute and I adored them. We strolled along the pathway that ran between two rows of houses. Most people here tended gardens of cactus and verbiage, edged by scented shrubs.

"Since I went to Talia's seminar, and met this woman, the professor, I have felt unsettled. We need to talk about it." But my husband missed the last part of what I said, lunging forward to grab Ben and stop him taking hold of a sabra leaf. Sabra cactus plants grew profusely. Grab a fruit or one of the swollen leaves and you had thorns in your fingers for days. I tried one more time. Alan, the father of my children.

"I need to talk."

"Of course," he said trustingly. We knocked on the door of Eli and Talia's house, and went in.

§

Their open plan living space was eerily quiet. A giant Lego house in one corner. A plastic garage under the heavy glass-topped coffee table. On the deep cushioned four-seater green sofa - bought from Danish Interiors in Tel Aviv - sat Professor Conway-Brown, reading a book. I was not close enough to see what book. Did she pluck it out of her bag, or had she already been into Talia's study? Lucky Talia having her own study.

"Hello!" I said brightly. The Professor held the book close to her face and peeped over it.

"Talia and Eli not here?" Alan asked naively. She pointed to a closed door, their bedroom.

"They are talking, I gather." Ben and Tom made a beeline for the Lego in the corner, and set about dismantling the house.

"We might as well sit down," I said to Alan. There was only one other chair in the spacious room. It was opposite the sofa that held four, an even lower one, on which Alan now sat. I positioned myself at the end of the sofa. Angelina put down her book. Minutes passed in silence. It was a warm afternoon. Then the door opened.

Eli looked white with anger and dark with gloom. His shirt was tangled, his hair fell forward over his brooding Israeli face. What was going on? Next thing Talia emerged dancing forth out of their bedroom, and burst into song! She wore a broderie anglaise blouse which billowed around her. She sang out from the finale of Verdi's Requiem.

"Libera me! Libera me!" Release me. "Oh, Anna! I forgot that you were coming. Hello Angelina. Sorry for the delay. But you know what they say – when there is an epiphany, there is an epiphany. No way to avoid it. I would like to tell you all that I have just made an important decision."

"Shut up, Talia. For sake of God in heavens get some drink for our guests," Eli spoke good enough English.

"I wonder how many families live in this moshav?" Angelina asked. A question, I thought designed to rebalance the moment.

"One more than there will be soon!" cried Talia. "Because we will have to leave Yadda soon, simply have to!"

"No we won't," Eli looked at me as if for support, a look of despair and hope both, and wiped his forehead blankly, as if life had suddenly thrown chaos at him. The metamorphosis of one harmlessly unconventional wife into an uncontrollable force of nature. Talia switched to Mozart's Exultate, Jubilate. She had an excellent voice. Angelina picked up her book again.

"Where's Noah?" Alan asked coolly.

"Ah, my little motek," half sang Talia, turning to look at us as if we were entirely new creatures in her world, "Noah wanted to go play with his new friend Margaliti. So we took him. Such a big boy now, so he learns to choose his own friends. So sweet!"

"But Talia, the twins were expecting him to be here. If we had invited Noah to our house, and the twins were expecting him, I would not let them just go off somewhere else. Actually."

"Well then, actually, we need to conclude that there is something completely amoral about me, something undisciplined, wild, something that today seeks inner integrity above mere out of date could I say English manners! Or maybe I am just one very rude Israeli!"

"I'll get Noah," said Eli hopefully.

"Lo! Don't do that!" she reverted to Hebrew. "Listen. Takshivu! Today is a turning point for me, and I will not be afraid to share this with you. Witnesses. Friends always, I hope!"

"But Talia," I sounded like my old head mistress, "you are being rude." A long pause.

"Because, Anna, something amazing has happened here. It would be dishonest of me to pretend my life can just carry on. Something in me changed today."

"What changed? "Alan asked frostily. "Are you able to explain?"

"Today I looked into my heart, and found – inner fury, yes, and loss, yes, and those dark sacrifices of my grandparents, yes! I tried to calm myself with study – and for an hour immersed myself in reading. But I became more and more vulnerable! I became," she reverted to Hebrew, petsa patuach - an open wound. "The aching souls of those great men, Beckett, and his mystical mentors, Proust, Joyce, all, they called me, or darkness itself called me. It was a moment of shock and existential terror, in which I came face to face with my own inner self. I am explaining the unexplainable. Listen. You have to listen. I rose above it! That's what I'm trying to tell you. But I need to get away now. I need to travel, to learn, to develop. I have to do this. I will collect Noah, and tell him how disappointed you are. Either I'll be leaving Yadda soon or we both will, Eli and me together with our son. We have a lot to decide. Eli will have to understand."

And out she went. The effort Eli must have been making to hold himself together. I wanted to go to him, hold him.

"Guys," he said, "I'm still here. Can I get you all another drink?"

"Best I should go." Angelina stood up carefully. This scholar of international repute.

§

Back home, we got the boys ready for bed. "I've never heard someone sound so dissatisfied," I said quietly, as Alan and I watched them in the bath, taking it in turns to stream water down each other's backs."

"As dissatisfied as you?" he stared at me.

"I'm not dissatisfied," I lied, "at least not with you. But I do wonder whether Yad David is the right place for me. For us. I've tried to tell you."

"What do you want me to say? Coming here was a mistake?"

The boys came squealing out of the bath and we bundled them in towels. Soon they were in pyjamas. They were so trusting, looking from me to Alan, knowing we were their parents and always would be. I was defeated by how reliable we were. Later, in bed Alan and I turned to each other and made love. It was all right. It always was. But tonight, as I was swept away by that deliciously dangerous current, which was not really dangerous at all, I got a shock. Alan's face suddenly wasn't his. Whoever the body belonged to that was warmly inside me, and welcomed with all my heart, the face I saw through half closed eyes, turned into Eli's. I blinked at the warm dark night and came again.

§

Two years later, as Talia and I strolled in the orange grove for the last time. I confessed.

"I had to look up the word, you know, to be sure of its meaning. Epiphany. James Joyce lifted it from a religious meaning to a literary one. That day, I didn't feel sorry for you. I felt jealous of you. I was born and brought up in English. How could a word like that have escaped me?"

"Trust me," Talia laughed, "I'll never tell."

Alan and I left Israel, Talia and Eli left each other, in that same year. By the time we packaged our belongings in big boxes, which travelled with us to Manchester along with our suitcases, they had separated. Eli found a teaching job in Sweden, and set about commuting between Israel and Scandinavia. He fell in love with the Norwegian Fjords.

And Talia? Leaving Noah to take up residence with his grandparents in Rosh Pina, a small town close to the Lebanese border, she flew off to India. We learned this in our final meeting with Eli, whose distraught face continued to appear to me in the dark at unexpected moments, but didn't seem to be doing me or our marriage any harm.

"She is the walking wounded," he generously defended his wife, who before leaving for India had an affair with a lift engineer from Ashdod. They met on the beach. Best sex was at twilight, as the sun dipped into the Mediterranean. Or so Talia told me. Epiphany or not, Israel had proved too much for me. So had the friend I would forever associate with growing up and looking to new horizons.

§

1993: I am standing by French windows that open onto a lawn surrounded by rhododendron bushes. It is May, they are in flower. Sublime pinks and purples. There is the hum of bees.

I am in a house in South Manchester, here to give a talk. "My Years in Yadda," to a Zionist women's group. The women assembling to hear it chat quietly in the carpeted lounge. I check for numbers. Twenty. Andrea Cohen brings me tea in a porcelain china mug. "To Their Highnesses Charles and Diana on the occasion of their wedding."

"So tell me," Andrea asks loudly, "what made you leave Israel, and come back to this god-forsaken country?"

It is not my intention to overreact but something takes hold and I feel critical of this group. It is already a few years since we left Israel and I am still enjoying exploring Manchester. Alan's great grand-parents arrived here in 1885 as immigrants from Russia. His parents, elderly but healthy, live in North Manchester, we live in South. Manchester was the cradle of the Industrial Revolution, and movements which have propelled my adult life, from Zionism to feminism have roots here.

Not my intention, or perhaps it is. Perhaps it has been dormant in me since the day of Talia's Epiphany – the urge to emulate her, stake my own claim to daringly independent thought, tread a path to existential freedom. Don't be ordinary - stand up and speak.

"I do not consider this to be a god-forsaken country any more than I found Israel to be one. Actually." The women are all in high heels, I am in trainers.

"Let me take your cup," says Andrea Cohen gently, then whispers, "Sorry. I didn't mean it that way."

"Maybe," I say coolly, "but it has made me stop and think about what I mean."

"Do sit down," she instructs her Zionist ladies, "so our speaker can speak." Then, "What are you doing?" she says urgently. I'm tearing up my notes, scattering them on the lush carpet.

§

"What is the meaning of where we choose to live? You say Israel is the best place in the world, but you say it in Manchester."

"I am simply curious," someone insists, "to know why you left Israel, because for us it's the dream. To get there, to be there." A group sigh. They all feel the same.

"Language, identity, culture, and my friend Talia didn't help!" Now I'm laughing. "Though perhaps I should put my crazy friend top of the list!"

I begin to describe how Alan and I arrived at Yadda and I found an instant understanding from Talia because of her love of English literature. Something about building cultural bridges, I suggest. I include how Talia and I drifted from English to Hebrew and back again, or the other way round and it made no difference. But as I describe walking through orange groves with our toddlers in tow, and the women keep murmuring oh how sweet, how gorgeous, I begin to bristle.

"Look. Israel is complex, new, forming and re-forming, confusing, annoying, liberating - depending what you want to be liberated from." That should stop them in their tracks. "And what happens there happens in a dozen languages. Not just Hebrew. Arabic, French, Russian, Portuguese, Ladino, Yiddish, German . . . I could go on."

But I don't. I'm thinking that it's impossible for me to sum up a whole country in half an hour and it is a mistake to have come here at all. No, they insist, just tell us. We love hearing. After all. Eight years. It must have been like a dream. No, a dream come true. All that sun. And hummus and falafel, did you eat lots of it? And did you see olive trees growing?

"We have a holiday home in Spain," volunteers one woman, trailing her long hair across her cheek, first with one hand, then the other. She sounds like the Queen, and has a sweet face. "It is surrounded by olive trees. Every time I go there I dream of Israel."

Is that the statement that catches my attention? Is that what makes me think of Talia's aunt? Her South African aunt Shirley, who had the softest voice I had ever heard, as well as long soft hair. It's the uncritical adulation, the worshipping of this country none of them will ever want to live in and that we chose to leave. It's pie in the sky, it's the heavenly Jerusalem. For God's sake.

My friend Talia had an aunt in Ashkelon, I finally begin, and twice took me to visit her. This aunt who was called Shirley lived in a neighbourhood called Afridar - an acronym of South Africa backwards in Hebrew. And Shirley took us to what Talia called jokingly the centre of town. With her soft South African voice, you had to lean close to hear. Then I tell them what Shirley told me. And my voice goes lower as I speak - quieter and reflective.

"The buildings we saw, shops made out of old houses, the Ashkelon social services department – all these were previously houses belonging to the Palestinian people of Majdal, which had now become Migdal. Arabic to Hebrew. The easy switch. In Ashkelon, unlike most places they will have heard about, the Arab population stayed at home, didn't run away when Israel came into being in nineteen forty-eight. But they were thrown out, basically, in nineteen fifty-one. Yes they were. Put unceremo-niously in lorries, and driven to refugee camps in Gaza."

I am carried away. I draw breath, get a grip. Finally I recall how once a month my old friend Talia took her little boy, and went to demonstrate with an organization called Women in Black, women who protested against the Israeli occupation of the West Bank and Gaza.

"More tea anyone?" Andrea Cohen tries to get a grip on the stunned room. They look at me as if I ought to be stood against a wall and shot. Me and my story. Andrea circulates, and fills porcelain mugs with fresh tea. The teapot is antique, coated with tessellated leaves, with a gold lid. I think of history. British history, Jewish history, Palestinian history. Truth. Have I done something wrong? It feels like it. Of course, I say now, my friend Talia is Israeli to the core, but like me she hates the policies of successive governments. Although, I now add, it has to be said, and in my opinion this is crucial, the real reason she took herself off, first to an Ashram in India, and later to where she is now – high on a mountain in Costa Rica - has nothing to do with politics. It is more, I say a question of personality. Yes, in her case I would say, only personality. I add that she is intensely literary.

"After all," I say to the ladies of the lounge, who I now realise consider me somewhere between deranged and dangerous, "Those who study literature to any depth know we are all intrinsically multifaceted." Two people stand up to leave, one with a loud click of a handbag. Another retorts on her way out: "Well! You'd make a bloody good ambassador for Israel!"

§

2003 A decade later. The twins are students. Ben doing a degree in History and History of Art. Far away from anything either I or Alan might have done. Tom in Geography and Business Studies. They seem happy.

Other big changes. When Tom and Ben were thirteen, my brother Martin and his family told us and our parents that they were packing up in London and moving to live in Jerusalem. My parents were determined to support him. There had always been Zionism in the family.

"Years back," my mother said, "I was sure you and Alan would settle there. In fact it was our intention to buy a flat, follow you there, end our days near you in Yadda. But now, we will go, and we'll be near Martin and his family." Alan said nothing for three days after they told us this. He was more sorry than I was about leaving Yadda and Israel. But we promised to stay close - all of us. We sent them on their way with hugs and a promise to visit.

And my brother's first year in Israel happened to be the same year that Talia came back from Costa Rica. At first, when she got back to Israel Talia wrote to us describing her adventures. One saga involved a German scoutmaster, another a Dutch Buddhist who had previously been a physicist. On our second trip to Israel to visit Martin and my parents we spent the first evening with Talia in the tiny flat she now rented in Tel Aviv. Eli was in Stockholm with his Swedish wife. We hugged each other, marveling at how many years it was since we'd spoken. We took her to one of the new restaurants that were springing up all over the Tel Aviv Marina and treated her to a real meal. Hummus, salad, shish-kabab, chocolate gateau.

"What are you doing tomorrow?" she asked us.

"Tomorrow," I replied, "we're seeing Martin. Then my father has a doctor's appointment. I promised to be with him. He may need a hip replacement."

"The day after?"

"Taking our niece to the Safari Park in Tel Aviv. Lions and tigers."

"Not really much time to see an old friend, then."

"Excuse me? We're here, now, and it's wonderful."

"But from now it's only family, is it? You need to be seeing all of them. More of them than me. Obviously. In which case . . . goodnight. Laila Tov." She upped and left.

I stood on the wooden decking of the Tel Aviv Marina, the thud and swish of the Mediterranean beneath me, breathed in the salt spray.

§

A year later, I made sure to contact Talia well before our visit. We knew by now she was short of money, and things were bad between her and her parents, who still had Noah. He no longer wanted contact with his mother. He preferred visits to his step-mother in Sweden who treated him to football scarves.

"Dearest Tali," I wrote, "we are writing to invite you to come and stay overnight with us at our hotel by the sea. That way we will have a whole day and possibly a morning, for catch up and chat, before we go to spend time with my parents and my brother."

"Dear Anna," she wrote back, "If you really cared about our friendship, you would understand that one night in a hotel with you both is not enough. Two or three - I might consider." So on that visit we didn't see her. Nor the next one or the one after. Tom and Ben left university and found jobs in London. Very occasionally we heard from Eli. Noah moved to New York, where he met his soul-mate Yossi. By day they worked as delivery boys, and at night they trained as Tango dancers. Go figure, Eli wrote.

Shortly after this my father died, and we spent a whole month in Israel, grateful to be there for the week before he passed away. During the Shiva I called Talia nine times, and left five messages. I hoped she would relent and come to see us. But she didn't.

2008: It's almost dark, the longest day of the year. We have been chatting all day. At last. What is friendship, I ask myself? What is success? What is happiness? I'm still reclining on a garden chair but Talia has slipped to the ground, sprawled on the grass staring at the sky, which is beginning to twinkle. In Yadda the whole moshav was our garden. Here we have a back garden. The boys played cricket in it, in their teens, and it has memories of what Talia envies. Our long-lasting marriage, the close family.

"You have everything now," she says. "Me, I have nothing. Your leaving Yadda was the nail in the coffin for me. I have no money. Noah spends more time in New York than Israel and we hardly speak. Weeks go by. My heart is permanently broken. Yours isn't. Your boys. They phone you every week."

"Er . . . sometimes they don't. But when they don't call me I call them."

"Noah doesn't pick up when I phone. In any case I can't afford it."

Alan has gone part time and runs a dental clinic for children with learning difficulties. He is immensely patient with these children. Securing his place in the world to come, he has joined the Samaritans and goes off one night a week to sit in a small office waiting for calls from desperate people.

"Me, I have nothing," Talia repeats.

"You've had a successful career," I remind her, even though I know from Citizens Advice that when someone tells you their life is a mess you don't urge them to look on the bright side. She has taught at some excellent schools. During the years when she wouldn't talk to us at all, one of her students won Best English Scholar of Tel Aviv. I knew this because it was in a photograph in the overseas edition of The Jerusalem Report. Alan has it delivered weekly.

"My last job," she said, "they sacked me."

"Why?"

"Two stray cats turned up. My students decided that the difference between domestic pets and so-called wild ones was an injustice. They created a haven at the edge of the school grounds. But then there was a rabies alert all over Israel and we were reported. Two malnourished cats! The animals were taken away and I was sacked. Crazy."

And me? If I stop to reflect where my impulsive love of English literature, language and theatre led me, the answer is - nowhere. Or nowhere that counts in anyone's dictionary. When we first came back to the UK, I began a degree at the Open University. English Literature. But I ran out of enthusiasm and failed to finish it. Eventually, using the languages of my first degree, I took up private coaching for school-children. It fitted our lifestyle. German, Spanish, French, I did it well enough. These days I am an advisor in the local Citizens Advice Bureau.

§

"Was it good for you, in the end? You have everything you wanted."

"Are you really unhappy?"

"I want someone to love. All I have ever wanted."

She stays another week. It's hard to fill the time. The more we talk the more there are things I can't or shouldn't share. This trope plays itself over and over. I have so much, she has so little. The only thing she has had far more of than me – is therapy. My meagre year in one-to-one and six months in Citizens Advice group training, these stand as nothing compared to Talia. She has been exploring her inner angst for thirty years, and I can't help it – I envy her for it! Talking to her, I sense that inside me there may be riches to be mined, if only I had the inclination to mine them. I remember Eli saying he wouldn't recognize an existential crisis if it hit him in the face.

One afternoon I take her out to lunch. Then we wander round the largest book shop, floor to floor. So many books, I am overwhelmed, engulfed, but Talia takes them in her stride. She skips from one display table to the next, talking loudly, and engages a bookseller in a discussion about intergalactic travel. As I drift from philosophy through poetry to psychology, I hear her calling, and she flies, yes flies across the wide floor of the multi-storey bookshop, book in hand. She comes so close, I flinch at the sun damage on her smiling face. She thrusts a book into my hands. "The Adventuress." A Novel by A C Brown.

"How on earth did you know what this was?"

I've known for a decade," says Talia, "that Angelina wrote a novel. She told us in seminars, "When I retire I will do it." Not long after we left Yadda she went to live there, you know. She married an Israeli artist in the end. And she says in the introduction that the adventuress in the story is derived from her own great grandmother. It's the story she told us. The girl from Jaffa. Here. This is your present!"

"You always had a talent for noticing originality in people! I just thought she was an academic."

"People are always more than one thing," she says. "All people."

"When we were young, in Yad David, what did we really know, of ourselves, of the world?"

"I have no idea," she says, "but I see this bookshop has a café. Herbal tea with honey for me."

This night should be her last night with us. Once again we sit in the garden, and it is no longer midsummer. The nights have drawn in by several minutes.

"Whatever we saw then," she is speaking Hebrew now, "I look up at the sky and see a huge number of stars! Have you got a sleeping bag? I could spend the night on your lawn!"

"You know" - our thoughts are not on the same tracks the way they used to be - "the Israel you live in is not the place we once lived. Sometimes our sons don't even tell people that we lived there until they were eight. Too many ask, how could you live in such a place."

"I have a new therapist," she says, "I couldn't leave Haifa now. Gila gives me new ways of looking at myself. She was Jungian, but she branched out. Perhaps you will come over, come to one of her weekends? Or better still," - she sits up, urgently – "come with me to a demonstration. There are so many people like us - or me - lots of us. We still demonstrate every Friday." A wave of nostalgia. Us as young mothers. Friday afternoons.

She leaves a few days later, and I am relieved. She never understood about routines, even way back when the children were tiny. She didn't seem interested in us, either of us, though we tried to understand.

The day after she left, the house is quiet. Life without Talia around is peaceful, less challenging. The life we have grown into.

§

2016 Alan and I have bad knees. Our bodies have grown old side by side. We cling to the wobbling rail as we descend from the plane. In the taxi to Jerusalem we ask the driver to stop, so we can get out and move our legs a little. Alan fishes Paracetamol out of his bag, and we ask the driver to stop again, find somewhere where we can get water. "We'll both end up having knee surgery," my husband predicts.

We rarely see Talia now. Two years ago my mother passed away. I flew back and forth, to attend her in her final weeks, and to pay loving respect after her death. My brother is growing old like us, and our sister-in-law is unwell. On visits now it is hard to explain why we want to take two whole days, hire a car and drive up to Haifa where Talia has finally settled.

Then one evening, as I sit on the veranda of my brother's Jerusalem home, he looks up at the sky. His head tilts back, his skullcap falls off and he bends to pick it up. He looks up again and points.

"Did you know?" he asks. "More than five hundred million birds a year fly over Jerusalem? That alone makes this city special."

"Birds," I say, and have a flashback to my undergraduate days - a student performance of The Birds by Aristophanes. This gives me the idea.

"Martin," I say to him, "while we're here, I'm thinking we might go and see a play."

"What would a play be about?" my sister-in-law asks suspiciously.

"If they can enjoy a play in the vernacular," Martin says admiringly, "that means they have not forgotten all their Hebrew. And that is wonderful." So they approve immediately!

§

A week later we arrive at the Khan Theatre, Emek Refaim Street, the street of the ghosts, to see a new play. I booked with such excitement that I didn't ask the title. Now I read that it's a new drama by a

Nigerian writer about two women, an Israeli and a Palestinian who meet in Germany, fall in love and adopt a Syrian refugee baby. Hebrew with English surtitles.

"Bet she won't turn up," Alan looks round for Talia. When I contacted her, she first said that she would get a train from Haifa to Tel Aviv, then a bus to Jerusalem, and would stay with a friend here.

"Sorry we can't invite you to stay at Martin's," Years have gone by and I'm still apologizing. I have everything, she has nothing. But she knows a man - Yanai - who has a studio flat in an old house in Rechov Hanevi'im. The Street of the Prophets. A five minute walk from the theatre. In our brief phone conversation Talia suggested that after the play, we might join her at Yanai's place. But I told her we would need to get a taxi straight back to Martin's. I exaggerated his infirmity greatly.

Jerusalem is noisier, fuller than it was before. On the way to the theatre, the taxi driver asks where we are from. How, if we live in Manchester do we speak such good Hebrew. When we tell him about our Yadda years he demands answers. What made you leave? Why did you not come back? Muslims have taken over France, he warns us, and now they're starting on England. Two thirds of London is Muslim now and most of them are terrorists. Not safe to be Jewish there. Then an altercation with the driver of a lorry distracts him, and when the shouting is over (in Manchester nobody shouts likes this), he seems to have forgotten his dark warnings. Now he asks amicably, which is better then - UK or Israel? "My son likes Manchester United," he chuckles. "How do

I get him a ticket for his eighteenth birthday? Bit of fun for the boy before the army. They all need a bit, before during and after if possible." Then he brakes suddenly, and swears. "Kibinimat!" What language is that? The jolt of the taxi wrenches my knee.

"Wait," he urges, and pulls in. We see traffic on both sides, and police. Is this a terrorist attack? There seem to be searchlights and cameras. A crowd of onlookers. My world turns, Jerusalem turns. Butterflies, apprehension. Seriously though, it can't be a terrorist attack. No shrieking, no sirens, no gunfire. Just strident voices, high-pitched then low. And whose voices are they, then? It's a demonstration and it's outside the theatre. There are queues (or the Israeli equivalent - crowds shoving roughly) unable to get in to see the play. I ignore the driver's command to stay in the cab, push the door open, cross the road, and find a footpath through a forest of bodies.

I recognize Talia, bathed in light. Some TV channel has been alerted to this. Did she realise this was the play we were coming to? What was it she said on the phone? "I don't bother with theatre these days. More drama goes on outside theatres than in. The Occupation . . ." she said. She's been saying it for forty years.

This Israel, the country we came to, the country we left, is it really the heavy fist, the dark shadow, the malevolent occupier that Talia describes, as she takes the microphone and begins to speak. Look how confident she is. Look how free she feels. How free she is and always has been. Forty years of protesting and see how she has thrived. Her kaftan is orange, yellow, purple. She's a rainbow dancing. But near her people are starting to complain. It's been a long day, they want to relax, get into the theatre and see the play.

All those years ago. What was really going on? We respected Talia for her weekly demonstrations but did we once, either of us, ever take seriously that deep in the heart of the Israel we were going to leave there were these currents? What currents?

"Tali!" I shout, but she doesn't hear. She's speaking into a microphone. To one side someone is signing. To the other, a woman in a purple hijab translates into Arabic.

After all these years, I'm still envious of my friend! Now I want to be a visionary too! I want to have a vision! In what I intend as a gesture of lifelong friendship, I wave hopefully to Talia who is chanting now. It sounds like a Buddhist chant - not Hebrew, English or Arabic. A policewoman barks in Hebrew, and the crowd has to take sides. "People demonstrating - move down the road, or you will be forcibly removed. If you wish to see the play, please do come through now."

Alan clambers out of the taxi and hobbles towards me. He shakes his head disbelievingly at our old friend, who calls out to the world and is escorted gently away from the theatre entrance. People surround her. Two of them are a sunburnt couple, he bearded, she with white hair loose in the breeze, her silk headscarf dangling. It's a balmy night.

"I am a native Jewish Israeli, born in Jerusalem" - her words are precise, she is reading from a card - "I have come here to warn you all that our country is in danger! We are in real danger of a prolonged occupation, of the Palestinian people. The excessive use of military force against civilians in the Occupied Territories in the West Bank will do harm to all of us, for a very long time. Please hear my message!"

And what do we do? We branch off to follow the theatre queue. Soon we are within the walls of the old courtyard, about to go into the Khan Theatre and watch the play. It turns out to be a good one. The ending makes me cry. Afterwards, we congratulate each other on having understood almost all of it. We are pleased not to have lost our Hebrew.

Acknowledgements

"The Lizard" was written in 1978, "Granny Malin's Message," in 2020, "Verity Thomas," in 2021. The stories have been published as follows:

Tell It Not (The Shelter). *The Jewish Quarterly*, 1982
A Lullaby at Midnight. *Spare Rib*, 1982
The Saint on the Wall. *Stand Magazine*, 1983
Seventh Floor. *Stand Magazine*, 2013
Waving in the Wind. *Words for the Wild*, 2018
By Madeleine Black. *Stand Magazine*, 2018
From the Dining Room Table. *Momaya Press Short Story Anthology*. 2018
The Dressmaker. *Litro Online*, and *Didcot Writers Short Story Anthology*. 2019
Words. *Jewishfiction.net*. Autumn, 2020
The Emissary. *Stand Magazine*, 2022

Thanks particularly to *Stand Magazine*, and to my publisher, Sholem Gimpel

Postscript

In the forty years between "The Lizard" and "Talia", Deborah Freeman brought up three sons, trained and worked as a Psychiatric Social Worker, and wrote plays, including: *Candlesticks, Xanthippe* and *The Song of Deborah. The Song of Deborah* was translated into Hebrew by Avital Macales in 2016 and staged at the Khan Theatre Studio, Jerusalem.

Red Heifer Press

Publishers of Torah/Judaica, Survivor Memoirs, the Humanities,

Arts & Sciences,

Belles Lettres, Poetry & Literary Fiction

Print Font: Bookman Old Style

.